THE LAND OF GO

The Land of Go

Stories by

Lynne Barrett

Carnegie Mellon University Press
Pittsburgh 1988

The Land of Go

The author is grateful for permission to reprint stories that originally appeared, sometimes in slightly different form, in the following magazines: *Quarterly West* ("Out With the Crowd"), *the minnesota review* ("Inventory"), *West Branch* ("Moon Walk"), and *The Pennsylvania Review* ("Wampum").

This book was completed with the assistance of a grant from the Commonwealth of Pennsylvania Council on the Arts. I thank them for their faith and support.

Library of Congress Catalog Card Number 87-71458
ISBN 0-88748-044-6 Pbk.
Copyright © 1988 by Lynne Barrett
All rights reserved
Printed and bound in the United States of America
First Edition

CONTENTS

Inventory   11

Out With the Crowd   29

Realty   41

Wampum   65

Moon Walk   83

In memory of Jack Barrett

INVENTORY

"What do you think?" said the Appliances manager. "Cotton?"

"Nylon," said the other man. "The skinny ones wear little nylon bikinis. Maybe with 'Tuesday' embroidered on them."

They stood right below me looking up through the iron mesh deck of the Appliances stockroom. I had my thighs clenched. I relaxed; I kept counting transistor radios.

"This one's a kid though. What are you honey, seventeen? A baby. White cotton spankies."

I mouthed, "twennytwotwennythreetwennyfour," and marked 24 on the line for SKU 37079 in the book. They really couldn't see much looking up through the grid. And I decided long ago that looking doesn't count. I closed my big notebook and backed down the steps, my sandals going clink clonk clink, while the men watched.

"What are you, Patty?" the Appliances manager said, "seventeen?"

"Eighteen in September." I reached the floor. I glanced over at the other man, a delivery guy, a greaser.

"And anyway," I said, walking away, "anyway they're pink cotton stretch lace. You can see all of them you want over in Lingerie, you know?"

The Appliances manager laughed his laugh like a snore.

That's what they like, when you talk back. If I told them at home, my father would holler, my mother would cry. But you just can't bother to get upset; I learned that the first week when Mrs. Grissing taught me the job. "The store makes you wear skirts and climb all over God's little acres to count the crap they haven't sold," Mrs. Grissing said. "And when you've got your fanny up in the air crawling into those bins, of course they'll peek. Big deal." Mrs Grissing had worked for S. Kotch nineteen years. Every day her bra cut a deeper crevice into the fat of her back.

As I walked out through Appliances, all the color TV's announced "Jeopardy. Jeopardy. Jeopardy." The clock radios agreed on 10:30. I'd quit Appliances early.

I crossed the main aisle into Paints, but Eddie wasn't there. No one in Paints or Hardware. In Automotive I found Eddie cutting a key for a customer. The manager of Hardware and Automotive drank, so Eddie pretty much had to cover. Eddie was supposed to be his assistant in charge of Paints, but, as Eddie said, no one bought paint at S. Kotch. People just aren't cheap about paint. Eddie was sixteen, still in high school in Singac, a tall kid with bad skin, but he was the only halfway cool person in the store as far as I was concerned.

Another customer lined up holding spark plugs. Eddie shrugged. So I decided to take off and tour the store. Over on the Softgoods side I could look at the Fall clothes just in, though I really didn't want to go off to college in clothes from S. Kotch.

As I passed Giftware, I said hello to Mrs. Sabatez, who was dusting. Mrs. Sabatez, a thin Cuban woman, dusted all day.

"I think somebody looked for you," she said.

"Oh? Who?"

"A pretty girl," said Mrs. Sabatez. "The girl was pretty." She nodded at her lambswool duster.

Maybe Eddie was right. He said that Mrs. Sabatez did downers. I smiled at her and moved on.

The hardest part of the job was killing time. Mrs. Grissing and her sidekick Mrs. Main were union reps and they landed themselves the easiest job in the store. Every three weeks we were supposed to count all the Hardgoods, floor and stockroom. At the start of the summer I counted as fast as I could until Mrs. Grissing took me aside: "Babes, you'll hurt yourself, climbing those shelves like an orangoutang. Three weeks is what it takes so take three weeks."

Not that Mrs. Grissing ever climbed anything. She and Mrs. Main might estimate, might guess, might never look at all. If the count last time in the book was 12 they just put 6 and three weeks later 0. Once it was 0 it was always 0. They never seemed to grasp that our boss, Cherrybeth, and her boss, Mr. Wold, ordered from the books. Like the fishhooks. Cherrybeth sent me to Sporting Goods my first day counting on my own, and the book began with fishhooks. Every SKU showed 0 on the floor/0 in stock, 0/0, 0/0, 0/0 for pages. I found hundreds of fishhooks tangled on the shelves and cartons of thousands jamming Sporting Goods storage. And you should have seen the lures.

Anyway, after she got a load of my counts in Sporting Goods, Cherrybeth explained that, as union reps, Mrs. Grissing and Mrs. Main would be difficult to fire. She relied on me. Now the two old bags mostly used their Basic Books as lap trays for games of Go Fish in the Paperbacks and Records stockroom. I did inventory, which still meant slowing to stretch the books over three weeks. Usually I worked all morning and then hung out with Eddie in Paints mixing weird colors on the mixing machine.

Or, like now, I shopped. I'd crossed Jewelry and Accessories to the center of Softgoods, Juniors A Go Go, where all day tapes played and a sort of mini-lightshow cast pink and purple amoeba shapes onto the clothes. In June I bought three psychedelic nylon dresses with front zippers here on my discount, to wear to work. They were cheap, and at the end of the summer, as my mother said, I could just throw them out.

Suede minis had come in, not bad if they were real. I touched them "hunntwothreefurfi — " This job got me counting everything. Even reading, I would find myself turning the pages, just counting them. Numbers blurred through my mouth "leven twel thirdeen furdeen fideen." I counted in my sleep. I dreamed "furdysevenfurdyeightfurdyniiiiine fiddy" till I woke myself and lay restless and ready to cry.

I used to be the only one in my family who didn't talk in my sleep. If I woke at night the house was full of noises. My older sister Maureen, before she ran away, would sing, my mother would cough and mutter, my father was always swearing, always angry, "Bastards all you bastards get you bastards!" But I slept quietly, until now, barely moving.

"Finished Appliances already, babes?" asked Mrs. Grissing.

I jumped. She stood under the slide projector, shifting back and forth to the music. I tried to think of a good reason to be over here, but she went on, "Well, great, because Mr. Wold wants to see you before lunchbreak."

She moved away from Juniors A Go Go and I followed. "Mr. Wold? What for?"

"Cherrybeth didn't come in today."

"I know. I thought she was sick." Cherrybeth hadn't come in today or Monday, but I knew she'd gone to the shore for the weekend, and Cherrybeth usually got a one or two day sunburn when she went to the shore.

"She's sick all right," Mrs. Grissing said. "She got married."

"Really? Which guy? The VW or the Mustang?"

"I didn't know you and Miss S. Kotch were so close." Last year Cherrybeth was Miss S. Kotch of New Jersey; Mrs. Grissing thought it was funny to call her that. Mrs. Grissing, as she put it, "didn't care for Cherrybeth."

Now, in the main aisle, I realized Mrs. Grissing was wearing a different dress than she started out with. This time I was sure. Mrs. Grissing was gradually trading her wardrobe for clothes from the store. We had to check our coats and purses at the Employees' Desk so we couldn't sneak things out, but the system didn't prevent outright exchanges. Mrs. Grissing had on some blue thing that morning — I'd guessed it was a housecoat — and now she wore a new check dress.

We passed Mrs. Sabatez, dusting.

"Keep up the good work, Señora," Mrs. Grissing told her.

"Anyway," I said, "so she got married, huh?"

Mrs. Grissing led the way up the interior staircase next to Cameras.

"So why does Mr. Wold want to see me?"

She put on her all-informed look and said, "I'll let him tell you, babes."

She led the way past Complaints, past Credit, to the Hardgoods office. Our office, Basic Books, was near the time clock and Personnel, but Mr. Wold was with all the big deals. Mrs. Grissing took the Appliances book, tapped on Mr. Wold's door, stuck her head in and said, "Here she is, Jeff."

I knew Mr. Wold by sight well enough to try to look busy when he walked by. Now he jiggled a chair close to the side of his desk for me.

He was thirtyish, with the kind of dip and roll to his light hair that was popular when I was a kid, like Troy Donahue. There was a combined baseball coach-and-math teacher in my high school who looked like him and some girls had crushes on him but I didn't. And Mr. Wold's nose was too little.

"Patty, as you know," he said, "Miss Jennings has resigned her position as manager of Basic Books."

I tried to look like I knew.

"I'm going to miss her — very much." He looked at me hard, then away. He started unbuttoning the cuffs of his long sleeve blue shirt and rolling them up. He said, "I am offering you a promotion to that managerial position."

"You are?" I'd worked there two months. I said, "I'm not very experienced."

"Cherrybeth — " He paused. I thought, there *can't* have been anything going on with him and Cherrybeth. "Cherrybeth recommended you. She praised your initiative. This will be a real boost to your career in merchandizing."

"Oh yes." My career in merchandizing was the line I used to get the job. No one wanted to hire for the summer so I stopped saying I was going to college, figuring I could just quit in September. I still could. It didn't look like Cherrybeth gave all that much notice.

"It's going to be tough," he said, "to replace you in inventory and I may ask you to help out with the counts for a while. This is our light season in Hardgoods, so I'll be able to break you in gradually with the order forms. Cherrybeth — " By now he had his sleeves rolled and he compared to see that they were exactly even. "She said you had done some forms for her?"

"Yes."

"So that's fine," he said. "If you'll stop in at Personnel they'll give you your manager's badge."

I started to stand up and saw that he expected to shake hands, so I did — his hand was warm and small — and kept standing. He said, "I'll be looking forward to working with you, Patty." I pulled my hand away.

"Oh my eye," he said, "my eye! I have something in my eye." He winked his right eye shut open shut and held it. "Patty, I've got something in my eye." I stepped over. His eye was squinched up so tight a fan of wrinkles ran up across his nose. "Ow," he said. "Will you look and see? Get it out. Ow!"

I tried to see. I smelled coffee. "Open your eye," I said, "and roll it around."

He took his hand away and opened his eye wide.

It was bloodshot near the corner, but I couldn't see anything in it. His irises were light light blue.

"Ow," he said, "don't you see it?"

As I leaned over, his right hand waved around and came to rest on my shoulder as if for balance. He rolled his eye and whenever my finger got close he shut it.

"I don't see anything in there," I said.

"I *feel* it. Must be an eyelash. Look close, I'll hold still." He opened his eye and looked way to the left, into his nose. And his hand wandered down to my breast. I thought it must be accidental, but as I tried to shift away he found my nipple and pulled at it.

I said, "Oh, I see it," and jabbed my finger sharp into the corner of his eye.

"Ouchouch*shit*!" Mr. Wold clapped both hands to his head.

"Got it," I said, looking at my fingertip which had nothing on it. I shook it over the trash basket and backed around the desk. Mr. Wold had his hands over his face. I suspected he was laughing.

"I better get over to Personnel," I said and closed the office door behind me.

Only as I wrote for the fifth time, Tierney, Patricia K., on the Withdrawal From Union Form SK-A-47, did I see: I had to be the one they promoted, because neither Mrs. Grissing nor Mrs. Main would quit being union rep to become a manager. I heard myself telling Mr. Wold, "I'm not very experienced." Stupid, stupid. "So stupid," I said.

Neither secretary appeared to hear me. The younger one was trying to get green tape to feed straight though her letter gun so she could punch out my name for my badge. The older one, opposite, was putting my forms into files as I finished them.

"Do I get my union membership fee back?" I asked the younger. "I only joined in June."

The older one looked up. "The grace period for withdrawal from union is two weeks."

"But it was $35."

"I'm sorry. But you won't have dues taken from your paycheck anymore; that's just like a raise."

"It doesn't seem fair," said the younger. She clicked the gun a few times, then broke the tape off.

"Don't I get a raise when I become a manager?" I asked.

"You'll be eligible for a raise at the end of the first six month employment period. That's the union schedule."

"But she's not in the union anymore," said the younger.

"Right, which means she isn't really entitled to their protection. They could make her wait a year. But the store honors the union schedule anyway. And meanwhile," the elder said to me, "you don't have to pay union dues anymore, which is just like a raise."

"I see," I said.

The younger one said, "EA or IE?"

I spelled, "T I E R N E Y," as she twisted the dial for each letter. She lifted the tape delicately between long white fingernails and attached it to the badge.

"Here you go," she said.

I took the badge and started to pin it on, but I got a weird feeling when I touched my chest, so I switched and put the badge higher up, near my shoulder, hoping they hadn't seen.

The older secretary read, "Miss Tierney   MANAGER Basic Books. Very good," she said to the younger, "congratulations," to me.

"Congratulations," said the younger, giving me a look.

When I left Personnel I punched out for lunch and from the refrigerator behind the Employees' Desk the guard handed me my paper bag. I bought a Wink from the machine and took lunch into Cherrybeth's office. Mrs. Grissing had left the Appliances book on the desk. Then I saw that Cherrybeth's Puerto Rico and Bermuda posters were gone. The office looked bare and new. Of course, the store was new; S. Kotch moved the branch here in March. Cherrybeth told me how, last summer at the old Newark store during the riots, all the men took hunting guns from Sporting Goods and held the store until the National Guard came to convoy them out. I pictured Mr. Wold holding a shotgun, his sleeves rolled up.

I unwrapped my tuna sandwich and found it had been

mushed. Mayonnaise saturated the white bread. I couldn't eat it. I threw it out. I sipped my Wink and sat at the desk. My desk. I started opening drawers. Order forms, carbon paper, blank pages to replace full pages in the inventory books. In the bottom drawer I found a cardigan sweater Cherrybeth must have left, and under it a pair of pantyhose with nail polish daubed around a hole in the heel attempting but failing to stop a run. Also a sample size can of White Rain hairspray and a roll of butterscotch Lifesavers with only three left and they'd crystallized. I threw out the hairspray, candy, pantyhose, and a broken comb I found in the center drawer. There was a hairbrush, too, and I started to pull Cherrybeth's yellow hair from it, then threw the whole thing out.

Then I got up, locked the door, turned out the light, huddled up in the desk chair. They always turned the air conditioning in the store so high the offices were freezing. I shivered and shivered, so I put Cherrybeth's cardigan around me. I could smell in it the old grapefruit smell of her sweat.

Then, testing, I touched my breast, to see if I'd feel weird again, and when I brushed lightly I did. Then I grabbed myself hard and it went away. No big deal, I told myself. Lots of guys had touched me. Mr. Wold was just the oldest. It would have mattered when I was fourteen, but not now. It seemed to me my life had been a progression of abandoned defenses, giving myself up in stages, kissing, frenchkissing, touching through clothes, touching under clothes, and when I went steady with Nick, everything. Which I'd thought was a big deal, but now that we were broken up, was it really? Just like kissing. When I was twelve I thought it was the greatest thing in the world that Barry Super kissed me, that he'd always be important. Well, kissing didn't mean much after a while, you could be kissed by just about anyone and take it. There were the slobbering kissers, the teeth on teeth ones, the guys who dug their tongues into the root of yours so it hurt, the nibblers, the lickers, the guys who started to talk and drooled down your throat; oh, I knew all about kissing. And how many guys had squeezed my breast? One two three. . . seven, and two weeks ago at that party Kerry Sterling, who hadn't called since, and Mr. Wold. Nine. What did it matter.

The thing is, if you're a girl, people touch you and think they've gotten something. Taken something away.

Certainly that's what my father went so nuts over, when Maureen took off. He took it out on me, wouldn't let me have the car, waited up. Just the other night after that party he grabbed my arms as I came in the front door. I thought he was going to check for needle marks — since he went to the police lecture on runaways he learned ten signs of drug addiction he always checked me for — but instead he hollered, "Do they touch you? Do you let the little bastards get their hands on you?"

The thing about Maureen was, she never dated. She was a groupie from the word go. Even early on, she would rather go into New York to greet groups at the airport than go out with an ordinary boy. So my father thought she was safe. And then she went to a Hollies concert and never came back. She sent a postcard from L.A. saying she was the girlfriend of one of the guys who *really* played the Monkees music and then she went to San Francisco and last time she wrote she said she was changing her name to Tenth Cloud. Which drove my father even crazier. But he always blamed some long-haired demon who had taken her while it was clear to me that she'd done it herself.

One time I went with Maureen to a monster concert in the Village: fourteen groups. It went on for hours with long waits for set-ups. Maureen flirted with musicians during sound checks and then while they played she danced in front of them, touching her hair, biting her lips. One singer with a platinum ponytail got her frantic: she bit and bit so close I thought she'd bite his crotch and I saw he was the pursued, the girl. In the months before she ran away, Maureen would come home from sneaking into discotheques and we'd sit on her bed while she told me that she'd kissed one or rubbed two's arm and look, here was three's sleeve, four's roach, she'd boast and boast, fisicksevunateniiine.

God it was cold. So cold I was hugging myself, shivering. I got up and opened the office and punched back in: exactly thirty minutes. I could always tell now when lunch was over. I took the Hardware and Automotive book downstairs and went to Juniors A Go Go, where I'd been when Mrs. Grissing interrupted. It was chilly here, too. Maybe it was true that they lowered the thermostat when Fall clothes came in.

In Juniors A Go Go I picked out one of the suede minis and a vest to match, together $26, and then a yellow crinkly gauze blouse, $12, which came to $38, with my store discount minus $3.80: $34.20, pretty close to my union membership fee. So I didn't feel too bad.

I took them into the dressing room and went to the far end, past the garment racks of layaways, and found a corner. I changed into my new outfit. The skirt was shorter than my usual, but heavy so it wouldn't ride up. It had its own chain belt, too; it was pretty nice for S. Kotch. I transferred my manager's badge to my new blouse, then pulled all the tags off and rolled them up with my old dress and Cherrybeth's sweater and stuffed them in a waste bin. I wondered where Mrs. Grissing got rid of her old outfits; I should ask her.

Instead of going back out I went through to the dock where Softgoods were unloaded. This was the core of the store, where all the stuff came into the departments. There were some guys down at one end eating sandwiches and listening to a transistor; they waved to me as I picked my way across. I climbed onto the Appliances dock on the Hardgoods side and went through the stockroom. My heart was slamming so hard I could see it lift and drop my badge, but no one would catch me.

When I came out into Appliances carrying my book, I could have been just finishing the count there, as I had in the morning, as if nothing had happened. When I looked at my reflection in the silver top of a stove I looked okay. It was a tough outfit and my hair was finally getting long.

The clock radios said 2:00. The color TV's showed nothing going on, just newsmen talking.

When I crossed the main aisle, I looked down through the departments. Only Mrs. Sabatez, way down in Clocks dusting, moved. No one else among the displays of Hardware, Houseware, Giftware, Cameras; all the inventory spread out waiting, cheap and unbought. The store was dead.

I crossed into Automotive. I didn't see Eddie so I sat in the Test Your Reaction Time desplay. It was a set-up like we had in Driver Ed. with red and green lights and a timer to measure how fast you moved your foot from the gas to the brake pedal at the signal. But here they'd installed it in a mock front seat, with a dial on the dash to read out your reaction time and a chart that told you what that was in car lengths at different speeds. They'd fitted it with S. Kotch car decor items: foot pedals shaped like bare feet, leopard terry slipcovers, a leatherette wrap for the steering wheel. Kids liked to sit in it and pretend to drive while their parents shopped, though they were disappointed it didn't move like those kiddie cars they have in front of supermarkets, that jiggle a while for a nickel.

I plugged in the cord to start the timer and tested myself.

I was always very fast. But then it's easy when you know a signal's coming.

After a while Eddie came out of Paints stockroom and noticed me. He said hi and came over and started playing with the am/fm car radios on their display. "What do you want to hear?" he asked. "Do you know I found a teensy little country and western station from up in Mahwah the other day?"

"Piss," I said. I'd gotten distracted and missed the signal. If I'd been going 40 m.p.h. my stopping distance would have been fourteen car lengths. I said, "Country and western in New Jersey?"

He started turning the display. The sample car radios were hung on a tall rack that had wiring down the middle of it so that they could be plugged in. Eddie was forever trying to catch some shy station with a 10 watt signal or pull in soul from Detroit, which meant he would move the display around Automotive, dragging the extension cords along.

"Where's your boss?" I asked.

"He's still out to yesterday's lunch."

Eddie was getting the Temptations. He started tuning all the radios in the same way. I looked at him: A tall kid with bad skin — or rather it was obvious that he had bad skin in winter. Eddie always went out at lunchbreak and stood against the concrete wall of the store and took the sun in his face, so now he was tan to the collar of his shirt and the scars only showed at his temples. He'd brought over some barbells from Sporting Goods to "build up his pecs" as he said, but he was still just as skinny as in June, in the white button-down shirt and khaki pants they made him wear to work.

It occurred to me that this was how I always looked at Eddie, and yet he was the only halfway cool person in the store. Early in the summer I'd suspected he liked me; he'd mentioned movies, but I'd kept it an on-the-job friendship. How silly, when I'd go off to a party and make out with Kerry Sterling, who never called. I thought, if I were a man and Eddie a girl, I'd look at him differently. The Appliances manager was turned on identifying underwear; Mr. Wold put on his act to fool me, just to feel me up; they'd think a kid of sixteen was meant to peek at. I tried peeking at Eddie. If I looked as he lifted I could see the damp shadow of his underarm. Was he wearing an undershirt? No. There was the line of his spine, clear through his shirt. He had a flat little ass. And when he turned I could tell his cock lay to the left.

Oh, you could do it to anyone, I thought. Why not Eddie?

Eddie said, "You'd probably rather listen to Cream or something."

I said, "Jefferson Airplane."

He smiled. "Maybe Grace Slick is one of your sister's friends by now."

I'd told Eddie about Maureen. He thought the name Tenth Cloud was great; he suggested cloud names for my whole family, Storm Cloud for my father and Rain Cloud for Mom and I should be Fog or Mist or Haze because I was all over the store.

"Oh, hey," I said, remembering, "I got promoted. I'm manager of Basic Books." I showed him my badge.

He asked what happened.

"Cherrybeth got married and quit."

"She was here this morning," he said. "Did she find you?"

"Cherrybeth?"

"Yeah, she came in when we were busy. She asked if you were counting Hardware."

"Mrs. Sabatez said someone was looking for me. I wonder what she would have said."

Eddie went to the counter. "Wait," he said, "she asked me — " He looked around the register and then went into Paints. "I was busy so — yeah, here. Good thing you reminded me."

He brought over an S. Kotch bag, the smallest size. Cherrybeth had written on it:

> Dear Patty,
>   Chuck and I are getting married this Sat,
> but I told them I already was so they couldn't
> hassel me. He's the one I told you about remem-
> ber? So now you'll be the only one in the store
> who can do fractions. You're one in a zillion,
> kiddo. Take no shit.
>   Cherrybeth Russo (to be)
> P.S. Don't run for Miss S. Kotch it's fixed.

I showed the note to Eddie. I felt better thinking she had tried to see me. Maybe she would have warned me about Mr. Wold. Sometimes she called him "Mr. Mold" I remembered. I wondered if he'd fixed the contest for her.

I said to Eddie, "Don't you think we should celebrate?"

"Your promotion?"

"Yes, my promotion. How often does a seventeen-year-old get to manage Basic Books or anything, huh?"

"Okay," he said. "Let's have a drink."

"Sure, a drink," I said. "But what can we drink?" I got out of the display car and started hunting around. "Quaker oil? Anti-freeze? Does Mr. Ellicott get into the anti-freeze much?"

"No," he said, "but he's got — come on." He led me over into Paints, into the storeroom, into the far back. "Did you forget these?" he said. "Mr. Ellicott's rock-n-rye."

We had found them a month or so before, a set of four pint bottles hidden behind a row of S. Kotch Interior Enamel. Mr. Ellicott had filled them with rye and put in rock candy crystals. Eddie said he knew other people who made it, it was a liqueur. We figured Mr. Ellicott had put them there in better days, then forgotten them.

So we sat where we always sat, on the bench by the mixing machine, and Eddie opened a bottle and we drank. It was rough and sweet and mixed with the smell of Paints stockroom, like the smell of everybody's basement on a rainy day, the smell of glue sniffing when I was twelve, before they took the high out of glue. We took turns swigging the rock-n-rye and toasting:

"To Basic Books."

"To Miss Tierney, Manager of Basic Books."

"To Cherrybeth Jennings Russo-to-be."

We toasted Mrs. Grissing, Mrs. Main, Mr. Ellicott, S. Kotch, Mrs. Sabatez. I had it in my head to toast Mr. Wold but couldn't quite say it. Eddie got up and put a gallon can on the mixing machine, just so we could watch it shake. He took a pair of paint mixing sticks and started drumming on cans of paint with the mixer as back beat. He played around the stockroom, rapping on my head as he passed by. Once Eddie and I talked about what would be the best song to have played at your funeral and he said he wanted "Knock on Wood" or "Grapevine," something with such a beat that no one would be able to keep from moving, including, maybe, him. Now he finished with a wipe-out solo on some primer and flopped down beside me on the bench and opened the next bottle of rock-n-rye. I found myself studying his khaki thigh.

"To Eddie DeSantis," I said. "To your career in merchandizing."

"My career," Eddie said, and drank. "Hey," he said,

"maybe they'll fire Ellicott and make me head of Hardware and Automotive. I'm sixteen, after all."

"Maybe they'll fire all the old guys and put kids in charge."

"To the first teenage-run discount department store."

"We can take over — "

"—have splash parties in the Children's wading pools—"

"—rock concerts in Juniors A Go Go—"

"When I'm Branch Manager," Eddie began his campaign speech.

"Let me tell your fortune," I said, and took his hand. He jerked in surprise, and as I held his palm and concentrated, I could feel a quiver in his knuckles, though he held still. I tried to recall, of all the guys I dated, whether I had ever touched one first. I had, when attracted, talked to them, waited near them, willed them towards me, but that first touch, crossing the distance, had never been mine.

"Well," I said, "what a nice long lifeline you have here."

"Oh good," said Eddie.

"And," I twisted his hand and looked at the side, "two marriages."

"Two?"

"One short and unhappy, one long and unhappy."

"Great," said Eddie.

"Well, maybe those are the lines for children, I'm not sure, I only studied this for a while when I was thirteen or so."

"So maybe it's two children, one short and unhappy, one long and unhappy?"

Eddie is cool, I thought. "It's not just the lines, either," I said. "It's the mounds."

"The mounds?"

"All the fleshy parts." I rubbed his hand, which was thin and calloused and had some light green paint on it. "There are ones for scientific and mathematic and artistic, but I don't remember which is which. But this," I squeezed the outer part of his hand, "is the mound of the moon. That's imagination."

"Do I have imagination?"

"You're very imaginative. And this is the mound of Aphrodite. Venus." I touched the flesh below his thumb. His hand was sweating lightly. Oh, this was fun. "It shows sensuality." I brushed his wrist.

"Patty?" he said. "Do you want to go out after work?"

"Oh," I said, "no. Let's not go out after work. Let's not date, no phoning or not phoning, let's just do stuff the way, you know, you hear music, you move, you don't have to think about it."

"Patty?" he said. "Are you okay? Are you going to get sick on that stuff?"

"No, no, I'm fine," I said, running my hand along his spine, each vertebra, through cloth, distinct enough to number, reaching down to where his shirt would end and I'd find skin.

OUT WITH THE CROWD

Going to the ballgame on this late May afternoon. On the bridge, the crowd looks up to check if the stadium is any closer — no, still half the river's width to go — and then they stare away and count their steps under their breath. If they can only hold off long enough, the next glance may find them almost there. They don't want to mind the slowness, don't want to spoil their mood, the going to the ballgame mood of lifting anticipation. And so they watch the river. Beyond the railing, brown water spreads towards the blur of new leaves in the park, the haze of heat hitting cement in the city. The river evaporates without horizon into the milky sky.

"A waterskier!"

One child spots him, calls out. All turn their faces and look, river air thick in their nostrils, summer something warm and promising that presses their cheeks, as a small boat heads straight towards them, towing behind it a tiny man. So far off, he is a poster, fixed, vertical, and glad.

The skier sloops along, his skin pricked by drops of dirty water, his arms numb, watching the trees rise in the park and the building like a big white tub — but that's the stadium. They have come too far. A ferry crosses here and soon they'll reach where the barges run, they should turn, they should turn, he should drop the bar and fall here, but the water will sting with acid, he fears it, and so powerless he skims on and on, and the bridge slides up to him. A flock of birds ripples the railing edge, no, heads, faces watching. *Have they come to see, have they come to see me?* He waves. They lift their hands and toss the wave back. He wobbles. *Have they come to see me die?* He waves again, *Remember me*, as he passes under, into a block of cooler air, as the water turns dark green, then light, as helplessly he slithers and sloshes, on and on.

The crowd lets him slip beneath them in silence, then some of the young men murmur about his madness, and all look up — they've forgotten themselves for a minute and now the stadium is much closer — why, they're more than halfway, almost there. They speed up, cross more eagerly, clatter down the steps onto the paving. Teenage boys in yellow caps shove each other. Some of them pitch invisible balls and some of them swing invisible bats. Dating couples, sweating where they touch, tangle arms and touch more. A family's wicker basket gets stuck in a turnstile and the crowd bunches up again.

Once through, with tickets in their hands, they begin to circle outside the stadium. Their long shadows lead them toward the gates, marked A, B, C, on tall pillars. After the A's, the B's, break off and disappear, the C's go on together till they too pass into the shadowy inner court, filled with the smells of hot spiced meat and mustard.

A man sells programs in the middle of the crowd. His voice grinds, "Programs, Programs, Up-to-Da-ate!" By a trick he has acquired he aims his stare at each forehead, just between the brows, so it seems to each passer-by his eyes are met and he must buy, yet the program man retains his privacy, can attend to the quarters warm in his palm, the paper slick under his fingertips, can think, snatch, dole. . . a woman stops before him, seems about to buy but doesn't and breaks his rhythms. His hands dangle and he says "Program?" noticing the blond down between her eyebrows. He feels her eyes in his and meets them, freckled green, but then the young man with her pulls her along and the program man patiently resumes his cry and the swift unfocussed circling of his gaze.

"You won't need it, Heather, I'll explain," the young man says as she looks back.

She says nothing. She is hot and half-mesmerized. The dense air curtains even Duffy's presence from her. Ever since they crossed the bridge she has felt that they are all enchanted, that though awake she must move with the sleeping crowd as it is drawn, is sucked toward something. Only the man selling programs seemed able to resist. But he is far behind now. As they stray on, past foodstands and souvenir carts, a noise inside the stadium excites her, a drone with a harsh rasping surface, the sound of shell pressed to ear, a low blood tide and crackle of cartilage, a whisper of skin.

Of a height, she and Duffy step with the same pace, though hers is sleepy, his eager. Her legs are longer, her stride in jeans more graceful; his thighs bunch with muscles under his cut-off shorts. He is wiry, nervous, curly-headed. The thick rubber soles of his Adidas slap the ramps as they climb. He is hot, too, but he finds the heat a goad. The ribbon patch on Heather's jeans tickles the damp hair on his thigh and annoys him, as do the broom ends of her braids where they flick against his arm. He checks the tickets and leads her through the dark entrance to their section.

After one look down, dazed by the swat of sunshine on the yellow seats, Heather keeps her vision limited to his back. The up-folded seats of their row push dangerously at the backs of her knees. Once tucked into place, though, she feels safe.

"I forgot the lousy radio," he says.

She replies that she is sorry. She looks around, watching time move on the waiting scoreboard, faster it seems than time should go in the slow hollow heat. Far below, the green plastic field sparkles.

Duffy moves in his seat, annoyed by the foolish comments around him; the remarks ("Stu won't play." "Saw these boys the other night. They're no good, no good at all this year.") are to him all stupid, all useless. Let the game begin, none of these words can matter, be quiet till it starts. The attendance, he notes, is disgracefully low, many blocks of seats still half empty. An announcer's voice choruses itself on three transistor radios.

Duffy repeats, "Should have brought it."

Heather looks at him, sees his annoyance, laughs. "We don't need it," she says. "Aren't we here in person?"

He shakes his head, yes.

"Am I being too spacey?" she asks. That is one of his few complaints. "I feel very happy to be here. I almost don't care if the game ever starts. Is that all right? Duffy?"

It's all right, he tells her.

And it is. He just wanted her to pay attention to him. He wants this evening to go right. His wife never liked ballgames and for the four years of their marriage he always went alone, after the first attempts to go with friends brought on jealous quarrels. Often he went to find a refuge and to think. It was coming home from the play-off game last year that he'd decided they must separate. His wife sometimes joked, on their better phone calls, that if the team had only won they would still be together. No truth in that. The play-off had merely finalized a thought he'd often had. Alone in the crowd that night he had been more aware than ever of his own smallness. When leaving, as he stood in the empty, trashy aisles, how piddling even his death would be, he thought, the body shucked like a wadded, sodden beer-smelling cup. He'd thought this, and wanted a hand to hold his, wanted the warmth of palm on palm.

Yes, but now he wonders, does a man ever know when he's well off? Hadn't he always enjoyed himself, during a game, alone? Alone he cheered, scolded, jostled, booed, drank beer. How many times he had, after all, walked home clear-headed and refreshed. He'd sometimes felt — often felt — after a game, that he'd been present at a piece of history, like witnessing a battle or the moment of discovery; the details would be recorded and repeated, studied and passed on. Everything counted. Averages would rise and fall with each pitch and swing, careers fold, records shatter, and he, Douglas George Duffy, would have been there. He'd have felt the pain rise in the knees of the famous base-stealer. He'd note the stuff the rookie pitcher had. Duffy supposed he saw a million useless things each day; here alone, every detail mattered. More, he mattered. His cheers, his boos, were part of the communal energy that moved those men down there.

He looks at Heather and wonders if he can quite let go in front of her. He realizes he was always self-conscious with Meredith. Even in their worst quarrels, even the time he threw all her flowerpots out the window, he felt his emotions falsified by her presence. Of course, it's different with Heather. He is pretty sure that he's in love with Heather. But still — can he be the same with her as when he was here alone? And if she constrains him, then will his share be fair, will he be able to declare (to himself, of course; Duffy is not a braggart; in after-game theorizing his comments are as deliberate and succinct as a bunt) his contributions?

Heather, now, as she scans the crowd, he feels to be remote from him, from him as one of them. But he does like her. He likes the way she wears her pale shirt open, the tan line showing on her breasts, as if, he thinks, she is happy with her body. Why shouldn't they be comfortable and close? He wants her to look at him again.

"Beer yet?" he asks.

She shakes her head, still looking across space. The loudspeakers announce line-ups as players chase each other onto the field. At each name a cheer rumbles in the stands behind home plate like the distant explosions of road blasting. The scoreboard flashes the names, the transistors repeat them. It's unfair, she thinks, pelting us with information, the same information from so may directions. A propagandistic teaching method. No wonder little boys retain so much of it. No wonder men can recite old batting orders and feel as if they're having a conversation. If only she'd bought a program, then she could ignore it all, knowing any fact she needed would be there.

To escape, she surveys the seats. The stands are almost full now and each block of them is minutely multicolored, fitted together like an old chintz quilt she had as a girl (she misses it sharply for a moment and wonders where it is, remembering its comfort, its endless fascination in the uncertain morning light, its ability to fill her mind and replace her dreams). The predominant colors here are blue, the faded chickory blue of denim, and yellow, the team color, although in the crowd it looks less gold than cream. Soft blue and cream. Uncomfortably, she realizes that she wears these colors herself, wears her fragile old jeans and a faded yellow shirt with its rolled-up sleeves and open neck showing her turquoise bracelet, her silver necklaces. But no one over there can see such details. She knows how she looks to those across from her; she is one small flower bud on one shadowstained patch of quilt, her head one speck in the dark speckled regularity of heads. As she watches, the squares bloom and puff up. Everyone is standing. Doll-men are posed at attention on the field. It is the anthem.

Heather too stands. She feels her heartbeat push against her palm. She turns to Duffy and sees again the wet curls and straight nose, the vertical lines his dimple has worn in his cheek. She feels, for the moment, very young and wondrous, and the girl she has been marvels that the woman she has become goes out with a grown man. A divorced man. His wife, to her, is a voice that can speak from the telephone and snap his mood, excite him, sting him, dump him into gloom.

His wife affects him more than she does, Heather often thinks, and even if the influence is painful, she envies it. She wants to matter most. When those calls come, Heather opens a book or runs water in the tub, and later she asks questions that imply she didn't hear. But, despite herself, staring at the page or watching the water race and foam, she hears his voice. The excitement she feels, listening to the sad and sometimes violent remains of an experience she hasn't had, confuses her, and so she withdraws. She is afraid for him to see her childishness. These are times when Duffy calls her spacey. She is grateful that he notices, that, more than other men, he seems to need her participation. She wants to matter most, but she has, also, the hope that she will do the harder thing and make him happy.

She touches his hand as they sit down, and he looks at her. She runs her thumb along his eyebrow, skimming off a fat drop of sweat which she carries, poised there, to her mouth and sips. "Sweet sweat," she says.

"You're nuts," Duffy says, and yet, happy, he hugs her. They lean together, and he begins to describe the game, adding his voice to the stave of information.

It is, the crowd agrees, a good game. They are standing at the seventh inning stretch, and a warm murmur laps among them as they review the play. At the start, the pitching was erratic. When foul balls sprayed over the stands, the crowd flowed together and spurted up to catch them. The third baseman hit his first home run since he was traded. The pitchers, finding their proper stance, the good warmth of the blood from shoulder to fingertip, the way to fill their minds with the steady voice of will, began to pitch beautifully. The crowd, in these early innings, applauded both sides politely, a good play being a good play, their love of the sport pure. Then, at their team stayed stubbornly behind, their mood changed. They began to respond to the organ and the low boozy tones of the announcer. At the seventh inning stretch they are still two runs behind. They are thirty thousand, forty thousand beers along, looser, and, with the cooling evening, more energetic. The friction of their talk excites them more.

The lights have come on, and Heather, standing, finds the crowd has paled to old confetti colors under the fluorescence. Duffy left a while ago to get a beer and isn't back yet.

"Hey Coke." "Hey peanuts." "Hey cold beer." "Ice cream. HEY ice cream." "Beer here. GETcha beer here." Clumsy voices call around her. She watches the hostile, blotched faces of teenage boys as they pass along the aisles. They look disdainful and unloved. She imagines they go home and press kisses into their pillows, unaware they have been watched by her, unaware of the grace she sees in their broad-boned shoulders bent to the weight of their cooler cases, their long nervous legs, slender hips wrapped in aprons, and small round butts.

The inning resumes. Duffy comes back to her. A vast exhalation rises from the crowd, thickening the air. A slow, careful inning, this one. The clock moves cautiously.

Heather drinks her beer, washing it across her tongue. She feels farther off from the crowd as its excitement rises. Duffy leans forward now and swears. She would join her attention to his, as she did earlier, but she is afraid to distract him with her questions. She tries to focus on the distant field. Its fan shape looks ceremonial to her; its geometric patterns, the diamond set with squares, the quarter circles, seem oriental, as do the formal neatnesses, the finicky brushing of the bases, the calculated changes in the ratios between the fielders for each new batter. The crowd watches each pitch in. The pitcher works with the concentration of a martial art. So elaborate, thinks Heather, so polite, like a coronation or a duel. Everyone keeping count of fractions of perfection. It is men who like such rituals, men who like such rules and protocols. They make up forms to contain their will to defeat one another, to determine who is less than whom. But as she watches the clapping of the tiers below, the strange exact unity of the movement becomes, although mechanical, exhilarating, too. She looks at Duffy as he claps and he falters, embarrassed. So she claps with him, timing herself by him.

Duffy feels miserable. His clapping is forced and hurts his hands, but he can't stop now that Heather is clapping along. What is she thnking about? Is she enjoying any of this? What does he know about her really? *Who are you?* They have begun the long slow task of trading memories. They have been patient over albums and yearbooks. He knows the ethnic backgrounds of her parents' parents, knows about her loss of memory in the fifth grade play, about the summer she turned pretty at the beach, about men she's lost and friends she's kept, he even knows she likes her arms kissed, but not her ears. He has slept with her, talked with her, laughed, cooked, bathed with her, staggered home drunk with her. She is a stranger. She doesn't trust him. For if she trusted him, wouldn't she stop clapping if she wanted to? If he trusted her, wouldn't he?

Heather claps. As she claps — perhaps it is the regular square rhythm — the game reminds her of an adolescent dance, one of many where she moved from corner to corner in the dark. Or, rarely, danced, her back wet with sweat where an alien arm pressed into her, her own body cold and unmanageable. She would retreat to the clogged air, powder sweet, tobacco warm, of the girls' room, where in the mirrored glare her orange hide of makeup frowned out at her. Always she was glad when it was over and she could ride home shivering as the night air cooled her, pulling her bangs away from her face. She withdrew from the talk of the other girls in the car, the teasing of whoever's father drove them home. How clear, still, the itchy weariness of her feet in stockings and then the peaceful anonymity of the night, the kindness of clean sheets, the gentle shoulder of the mattress, and the secret snuggling sex she shared with some dream sixteen year old or other. Then she was able to be beautiful, in her passionate imagination. But private satisfactions weren't enough. Always she went back, always, at the next dance, there she stood among the stacked cafeteria tables in the hallway. She felt smothered at the start of each new song, but she was drawn, back into the dark, to seek humiliation, to seek experience, again.

She leans forward as she claps and Duffy watches her. She has deepened, darkened. Her skin is a warm rose, her cheeks and lips and the rings of hair that escape her braids, orange. In the dusk, under the lights, the silver strands of her necklaces, each dangling a turquoise tooth or a coral claw, set off her intensity. He wants to let her know she is more important to him than the game. He adores her. He feels, he fights, memory's peculiar stubbornness, its will to acquire so different from his own. *Remember this*, he orders, *remember her, right now. Remember this.* The words become an incantation, adjust beat to the clapping of the crowd, and unconsciously he repeats them to himself as he loses the thought in the play far below.

Heather has ceased to notice the movement of her hands. She is watching, all around her, boys. She has followed them here, into their game, into their hideout. In front of her rows of them press forward, their elbows and knees spread, their shoulderblades moving as they clap. Yearning over the game, they are exposed to her detachment, giving their secret selves away. She glances at Duffy, like them so intent. With him, with them, she watches the field. She feels she must watch closely. Down there men play before the crowd, resolving all their dreaming into motion. She feels she is about to understand.

She claps. And Duffy claps, *Remember this.*

Yes, clap, damn you, the batter mutters as he walks up to the plate. Where will you be in August? Where were you last week? Yes, I'll wave my hand to you; that's right, cheer. *I'm the one you're here to see.* Yes, look me over, the one who reported overweight to camp. Thirty-two years old. Haven't I the right to eat? I sweat it off, don't I? I sweat it off for you. I sign my name to thousands of endearments. I mean them all. Keep them. Save them. *Remember me.* He hunches, the applause soaking into his shoulders. The pitch flows in and past him, grazes the bat, and skews back to where people leap to touch it. The hitter doesn't look after it, just crouches. Heather inches forward, worried over him. Duffy groans. Sometimes, the batter thinks, we reach a perfect understanding. Forget yourselves, now, give yourselves to me. *See what I'm doing? Remember.* Don't worry now, don't worry over that one, the next one will be good. Hush, he gestures, and the crowd is still. For him, they will the ball on, a nice pitch, a pretty pitch, a goddamn gorgeous pitch; with him, they swing the bat, twirl it easy, and feel the fat, voluptuous impact of the hit. *See?*

The crowd detonates. Heather and Duffy jump and holler; crowd Duffy Heather whistle twist jig spin whoop hug and kiss.

The sky is a deep Arabian blue, the river quiet and glossy, as they cross back. Duffy holds Heather's waist as they return to where the city shines, its oblongs of light spreading and distorting on the water. Beside him Heather's face and neck are faint, her hair feathery, her waist warms his wrist, they breathe in time, they walk together. *Remember this*, he is thinking. *Remember it all.*

Heather watches the moon, a round frail moon dented with blue. The hushed gossip of the trees is mysterious and painful. She is glad to lean on Duffy. His hand on her body is vibrant and reassuring.

Around them, people move across the bridge in loose clusters. Fathers swing empty baskets and carry children lightly on their shoulders. Couples, aroused by the softness of the night, try to keep the moon in view. When they get to the steps, the boys find shortcuts down the structural supports, dangling and sliding to emphasize their peril. The young men murmur about their madness or laugh and admit they used to do the same. The boys are full of energy as they reach the street and invent races and dares. Some of them pitch invisible balls and some of them swing invisible bats. The crowd passes into the city and takes busses for home.

On their bus, Duffy and Heather have to stand and cannot see each other easily. They contrive to touch elbows, though, and they listen to the conversations that accumulate around them, for some on the bus have not been to the game, and those who have tell about it importantly, backing each other up, and soon they become friendly, discussing among themselves the double play, the last home run, the chances for the season. Soon Duffy is lost in a dispute. Heather takes a seat when one opens up and kneels around on it to catch the gleam of the river as they go up the boulevard that parallels it. *But what about the skier?* Has he turned around, gone back to wherever the small boats dock? Has he passed on and on forever, from river into river? If his death in a crash is on the news, everyone will remember him, she thinks. But if not, *who else will think of him but me?* His image, having crossed our minds, must vanish. For fear she will never know about him, she begins to take him, in her imagination, back along the river, safe on the spray-wet seat of his boat, wrapping his blue-lipped body in a thick yellow towel, holding him till he stops shaking.

The men he has been talking to leave, and Duffy goes to her. Seeing her crumpled so, with her braids loosening and the back of her shirt creased and smudged, Duffy thinks she looks like a sad child. Then she turns to him and smiles, *who else will think of him but me?* with a brave entreating ugliness, and this is the way he is often to remember her, this image his memory takes, this moment snagged in one sure grab he keeps.

REALTY

A mistress gets used to resting on Saturday night. You do the laundry, take a long bath, look through the vacuum cleaner dust for your lost earring. It's pretty late and I'm lying across my bed doing a numerology thing I found in a magazine when this woman Cindi calls up and says I don't know her but her husband works with me at the Realty and is he there?

I say, "What would he be doing here?"

"I know he's in your bed. Richard, you bastard, you hear me?" she screams, really blasting.

I hang up on her and unplug the phone.

The numbers show I have no compassion. I guess that's right. When people start whining I just want to fly off. It comes out that I'm neat, though, and that's not true. I get up and look at my clean clothes stacked any old way on the closet shelves. I don't own a dresser. I never sort my socks. Maybe they want to be in pairs, though, in a drawer of their own, and I don't care enough about their needs, maybe socks fit under the category compassion rather than neatness. Maybe I should have added in my middle name.

I mush up an avocado with some yogurt and put it on my face and watch a horror movie.

So next morning about ten when I'm just getting going, in that stage when you've got clothes on but not ones you want to be seen in, here's Cindi pounding on my door. She's a mess, face puffy, eyes pink, would-be perky sundress drooping. She asks, can she come in and talk.

I say, "He's not with me. You should try the houses for sale. When these real estate guys want to get laid they take the girl to a vacant house they have the key to." I've been there, but never with Richard, who doesn't appeal to me at all. These young married men drink too much, come quick, and repent.

"Look, look, look," she says, "I'm sorry, Melissa, I know he wasn't with you, he came in right after you hung up and do you know what? He barfed on the bed."

"Don't be disgusting, Cindi, it's too early," I say, "cut it out. Tell me something cheerful and I'll give you some iced tea."

She says, "I took a shower and threw as much like hockable stuff as I could into the car and left him passed out in his own, um, I've been driving around for hours."

"Okay." I bring her into the kitchen and make us iced tea. From a mix but I put it in my mother's 50's metal tumblers that get misted instantly and numb your hand. I take the purple one, give Cindi the green. We sit out on the redwood deck.

She holds the cold aluminum against her forehead. I ask what she took.

"The silverware, the food processor, the toaster oven. You know, wedding presents. Bath sheets. I got the VCR but the TV's too big to move. A couple of prints—the frames were expensive." She rattles ice. "It's all junk really. I did take Richard's vintage comic books that he always says are worth a fortune."

"What about money?"

She makes a face. "I didn't want to go through his wallet to get the bank cards. But it doesn't matter. Richard hasn't made a commission in like two months. We've been eating out on credit cards, places with salad bars. The only cash I have is a wine bottle full of dimes."

She follows me into the kitchen where I make us tomato

sandwiches on whole wheat with a little fresh basil. I ask how long she's been married. Ten months. She's wiped out her sandwich like nothing so I make another and find some sesame crackers I took after an Open House for prospects. As we go back out I flip on the air conditioning. 10:45. Every day now it has to go on a little earlier and this is still spring; when the heat really strikes it'll run all night. I say so to Cindi.

"I like the heat. I moved here from Florida," she says. "This was my first winter. I used to go out sometimes and sit in the car with the heater on. That was the only place I felt toasty. Nothing is insulated here for when it drops into the forties, like you don't want to admit you have winter in Carolina but you do."

So I ask if she'll go back to Florida now and she starts to blubber. Everything she put into it, she gave up her last year of college, her Dad went like broke on the wedding, you can't get a decent haircut here, etc. etc. etc. I make more iced tea, vaguely listening to her through the sliding doors.

"What I don't get," I say, coming out, "is that everybody talks about these things as if they're an investment—you put in so much, how can you afford to take this loss. As if all your affection is stored someplace and you expect to get interest. But it's blown, it's gone. Do you think some new expenditure could justify all that went before? This is how people go bankrupt, this is how con men take you."

"What do you know about love?" she says.

Pretty agressive, for somebody I've had on my hands all morning. So I say, "Fine, Cindi, why don't you go inside and call up one of those radio doctors and tell him all this. Go ahead, use my phone." I take the empty cracker box away from her. She asks, may she use the bathroom and I show her where it is.

I change into shorts and a bikini top, spread a towel on the deck, and lay out. The sun comes right through my eyelids. My lips feel nice.

"This is a great apartment, Melissa." Odd tone. I know she's wondering how I can afford it. Executive secretary. Richard probably has her living in some dinky little hole. All his money goes on the salesman's front, the tanning parlor, dry cleaner, car wash.

"I wonder what Richard's doing right now," she says. "He must be worried." I laugh. She says, "You don't know Richard."

"Sure I know Richard. He thought getting married meant somebody would sleep with him every night without dating and there'd be bacon and coffee in the morning when he got out of the shower."

"What's wrong with that?"

"Did I say it was wrong?" I turn over. Cindi is sitting cross-legged on the deck. I tell her she'll get weird lines.

She straightens her legs. She looks a little better with her face washed. "I should be going. I only wanted to stop by and apologize to you," she says, "for my misplaced suspicions."

"Oh hell," I say. I just lay there for a while. I am in that state where you're not thinking, you're just saturated with light and heat, and the little loops of the towel are more important and comforting than anything than could be said. I can feel the backs of my knees go ultra-violet. I hear Cindi leave but in a minute she's back—I open one eye—with a radio and a pillowcase full of something that clinks. She takes out a silver candy dish and starts to polish it with a corner of the cloth. The radio, of course, comes on to beach music. That's a Carolina category. What they mean by it is: the Drifters. Some conjunction of music and climate has occurred here, the mysterious basis of religion. Drifters Cults. Over twenty-five years they've worked out strange elaborate dances no outsider can master. Clubs feature the Original Drifters, the Genuine Drifters, the One, True, and Only Drifters.

I say, "Cindi, I got stranded here myself, you know. The guy took off and I made the best of it. Women are like burrs, they travel by sticking to men and then getting brushed off."

No answer. It's time to get ready for my afternoon date. I drape my towel over Cindi so she won't burn and leave her there, asleep, her arms wrapped around her bag of silver.

Yow is a big name in this town. Yows have been here hundreds of years, but their recent good fortune began during the Depression when Mr. Charles Yow, Sr. bought up land so pitiful no one else would bid at sheriff's sales. He made money declaring he wasn't growing tobacco, used that for development after the War. Mr. Yow built the ranch house neighborhoods, the malls, the franchise strips that ring the city. When the Gas Crisis gave him a stroke, he retired. Charley Jr. likes to construct country clubs and apartment complexes. As his secretary I type agreements with lots of "herewiths" and "thereuntos" on my Selectric. Brown ink, parchment paper—Charley thinks I'm classy. I'm his mistress, or rather mistress of Yow Realty Co. Inc., since it writes off my apartment, it sends me along on trips to Hilton Head, it pays me a surprising salary for someone who can't take dictation.

If Charley Jr. divorced his wife he would lose his big house in Old Town, his daughter Charlotte who is eleven, his two-seater plane. The proposed downtown mall would be tied up in litigation, a shaky savings and loan might fall, the annual golf tournament would lose its chairman, and Mrs. Yow's project to make a park at the site of the Civil War raid might be abandoned. Indeed, the whole city would be affected. Who could want that?

So we work together and meet when we can. Today, in cotton dress and sandals, I am heading for a picnic in the country. In the parking lot I spot what must be Richard's car, the real estate man's four door, a Montego with the back seat full of junk. I make sure it's locked. I put the top down on my blue Malibu. It's the one thing I owned when I met Charley; I was living in it. Driving it always makes me happy and today I'm nearly crazy with the spring. Everywhere azaleas, dogwoods, fruit trees flowering peach and pink. As if some fabulous kept woman had thrown all her lingerie out the window. Not a mistress like me, who wears t-shirts to sleep in, but one of those fleshy babes from the 50's, flagrant, provocative, with the kind of breasts that would fit the magnolias' big white cups.

It's not my body that marks me as a wicked woman. It's my voice. My Yankee speech. After my first party here, a man followed me to my car, sure I'd been inviting. Why? I swore, I was sarcastic. Then the guy I cared for kept popping home, expecting to catch me fooling around, because my affection had a sardonic, unfaithful edge. I tried to reform. Tried not to shut words tight, tried to lift my declarations into quesions. But I've found there's always something, some irony in my vowels—who knows?—some otherness bred into my mouth, that implies that I am capable of anything. Why after all did Cindi choose me to suspect? I've gotten used to it. I even like the feeling that here among their foamy politeness I am free. And Charley says he loves my backtalk.

Sun baked shacks, cinderblock churches, the occasional fortune teller's red hand. Way out here in an unincorporated part of the county, I'm looking for Rose Briar Condominiums. Partway through the first twelve units somebody went broke and it got hung up between the developer, contractor, subcontractors, mortgage company and investors. Charley represents an out-of-state-bank—believe me he doesn't have any money tied up in it—and today he's supposed to inspect the project. I park beside his white Imperial.

The model home, curtains at the windows, azaleas by the door, promises a TV life of half hour mix-ups that resolve in laughter. Behind it, on bare red dirt, a row of likenesses stand mocking, unfinished, window openings wrapped in black plastic. I pick my way along hardened truck ruts. When I reach Charley he is squatted, squinting, looking, in his golf clothes, like he's assessing a tough putt in the wasteland. He points out the shape of a tennis court set out with pegs and string, stands up, puts an arm around me. We're both sweating.

"Ah don't like these condo's." He says it "con *dough*." I'm always hearing other words in his words. "They're not the one thing nor the other, not a family home, not a singles complex. Who buys them? Old folks waitin to die, couples headin for divorce. Misery boxes, so thin you can hear the neighbors bickerin."

"Apartment walls are thin, too."

"Yes, but honey, there you hear people makin *love*, it gives you *good* thoughts." I laugh. We walk back up towards the cars. "Ah missed you," he says.

"Oh, since Friday?"

"Yes, Ah did."

I like his "Ah"—it seems wide open, more generous and appreciative than I could ever be. All I know how to do is tease: "And here I haven't given you a thought."

"Well, Ah'll just have to remind you then." He grins and lifts a grocery bag out of his car. "Much *much* too hot out here for eatin," he says. "Let's picnic in-sad." He takes a tagged key out of his pocket and opens the door of the Rose Briar model home.

In the master bedroom, we are lying on top of the quilted satin spread. There are no sheets. No air conditioning—the electricity is off. With curtains drawn, shades down, the room is muffled, warm, and dark. I roll the cool, reptilian skin of an orange across my belly. I peel it, lean to feed a piece to Charley, and see he is asleep. His eyelids are jumping with dreams. I study the scar on his cheek made by a hot waffle iron when he was a kid. Old Mr. Yow hit him with it because he wasn't respectful of his mother's cooking. A pattern of five little squares, like a crossword puzzle. I kiss him there, then slither up to sit against the headboard and drink white wine. Strange day—everyone lapsing, drowsy. It reminds me of the summer when I was living in my car and always tired.

At first, I got no rest. Girls grow up on horror stories about the face in the rear view mirror, the deformed man who prowls with an axe. It wasn't till the third night, when I was a sleepless, desperate mess, that I hit on the idea of a used car lot. There, parked between one cream puff and another, I felt as snug and comfortable as one of those insects you see on nature specials, that disguises itself by resemblance to a stone or a stick.

I developed a routine. I parked in the used car lot around midnight and made myself wake by seven, before anyone came to work. I went to a fast food place and sat a long time over coffee, pretending I was grungy because I just got off night shift. In the restroom I changed into a bathing suit under a loose dress. Then I'd pick up a morning paper and go over to this huge apartment complex that had a clubhouse and pool. Whip off the dress, hop out of the car in a bikini, carrying beachbag and towel. Nobody questioned me; there were plenty of women who sat by the pool all morning. I even did laundry at the clubhouse. I'd read the want ads, swim, nap, then use the locker room to shower and fix my hair, dress properly. Afternoons I tried to find work waitressing—something where I'd get cash quick so I could move on. A couple of restaurants tried me out but didn't keep me. "You go bout twice as fast as you need to," one manager told me, "but you ain't *friendly*."

One morning I overslept—I remember lying in the back seat, listening to the little pennants flap, unable to rouse myself—till almost nine. I pulled out of the lot with a tire screech that attracted Charley Yow's attention as he drove by. Charley had an instinct for someone lacking sufficient real estate, he has said since. He followed me to the Burger King Drive-Thru—in some weird way I felt late for the pool, grabbed coffee—and right on to Pennyroyal Apartments. I changed in the car. I had done a few laps and was sitting on a towel combing my hair when he dragged a lounge chair over, sat on it sideways, and said, "Young lady, you don't live here."

I had my story ready: "No, sir, I'm a guest. My boyfriend's at work."

"Ah don't think so, unless the young man happens to work at B.L. Turrentine's Quality Used Cars—and don't tell me he's old B.L. himself because Ah know him."

I stared. He glittered in the sun, hair like copper wire, pale tropical suit, gold clip on his linen tie, gold watch, gold wedding ring.

"Ah believe you need an apartment," he said.

"Yeah, sure. Don't you think I need a job first?"

He yawned and sat back in his chair. Later I learned that lazy look of the realtor on a deal. The man could sell sins to the devil. "Ah see," he said, "you got a circular problem, honey. Nobody'll trust you enough to hire you if you have no address and nobody'll rent to you if you don't have a job. You ought to held onto the one thing or the other. How'd a smart Yankee girl get in this fix?"

"Trusting a southern boy." Maybe I was still on a soft edge of sleep, because I told him about moving here with Billy Ray, who, further north, had seemed affably rowdy with his Stars-n-Bars bedspread. Who imagined insults he had to fight out in parking lots, getting himself fired from every job he found. Who sulked for days when I looked for work. He wanted me to stay indoors half-dressed waiting for him and not fret about overdue rent. He called up one night to say he was off for Alabama till things cooled down and I should get out of the apartment, police might be dropping by. Little misunderstanding about fake credit cards. "You go on home now," he said.

It was a furnished apartment. I packed what I considered mine into my car and here I was.

"Why didn't you call home for help? Haven't you got family?"

"Not really. Do you know what I do at night? I listen to the car radio just to hear disk jockeys talk. Somebody decided all announcers should use the accent from between Buffalo and Erie—that's Standard American, did you know that? That's where I'm from. I listen to them and feel at home. I'm surprised you people aren't more affected by it. I thought mass media was supposed to homogenize us all."

"Well, Ah think most people would rather just talk like their daddy. Of course, those who get educated learn to be intelligible to northerners. Those who want to rise. It has its uses. In fact," he grinned at me, "can you answer the telephone?"

"Come on."

"Ah mean it. Say, Charles Yow Realty, may Ah help you?"

"Charles Yow Realty, may I help you?"

"Help yew," he mimicked. "That's just great. It's so *mean*. Honey, you got a job if you like. You can keep folks away from me."

"And if I have a job, I can get an apartment, right?"

"Oh hell yes," he said. "Live here if you like. Ah own this place. Fact, Ah built it."

I kiss across Charley's shoulders, trying to hit every freckle, till he wakes up. "What you doin, Melissa?"

"Connecting the dots. Charley? You remember that first day?"

"Mmmm? You sure were tan." He sits up and fishes for his clothes.

"Yeah, I'll never tan like that again. It isn't healthy."

He sighs. He has put on his boxer shorts and is turning his yellow golf shirt right side out. Something always gets into me when Charley's wearing more than me. I say, "You watched me, didn't you, changing in my car."

"Couldn't see much," he grumbles. "Just a lot of wrigglin around."

I cuddle into him. "Remember when you rushed me right off to see the apartment? You were showing me the bathroom, bragging on the all-built-in fiberglass unit?" He shifts a little. "And I said, did you mind if I tried it out, because chlorine was going to fade my suit? Of course, I was dying for a shower." I listen to his breathing. "And you stood there and watched me rinse off in my bikini."

"Right in front of me."

"You could have left. But you watched. Yeah, what would you have done, though, if I'd untied my top and taken it off, you know, to rinse it?"

He makes this little "hnn" sound I love.

"And then what if I'd just, oh, slid the bottoms down—"

He shows me.

Once Charley said to me, "It's so easy with you." Whenever I wonder about his marriage, I think of that.

I drive home happy. The air's so sweet I want to bite it. I try the radio, get a black preacher, a white preacher, "Up on the Roof." I laugh, imagining a state divided between Baptists and pagan Drifterites. Humming, I open my front door and see: Cindi has moved in. Her stuff is piled around the couch and she is standing in my kitchen with all the cupboards open, reading a cookbook. She gives me a big, "Hey, Melissa!"

"What's all this?"

"I wanted to make something special. I can tell you're a wonderful cook." She gestures at my jumbled copper pots. I brace myself for a storm of flattery before she gets to the point, but instead she crosses her arms and yells, "Where *were* you? I didn't know where you went or even if you were coming back tonight. *And* you left me here with all your things. You don't know me. I could have robbed you blind."

I wonder how her husband handles these attacks. I say, "Nah, I knew your car was nearly full. You couldn't take much. Cindi, why are you still here?"

"Well, of course I wanted to say thank you, and then I thought, if you weren't coming back I could like stay over here and drive to Florida tomorrow, you know, start fresh? May I please?" I stare at her. She says, "If I can't stay here, I'll go right back to Richard."

This sounds oddly like threat. I wonder, does she think I'm the sworn enemy of marriage? Well, maybe I am. I say, "Just so long as you get your ass out of here early. Come on, let's cook some dinner."

"Let's make something strange." She gazes into my cabinets. "I've never seen so many spices. Richard won't let me use anything but garlic salt and chili powder."

I remember once Charley told me that the only flavoring his wife knew of was pork fat. These past three years I have been cooking my way across Europe and into Asia for him, when he has an evening clear. Restaurants are risky. We're discreet. Some people have to know, like Jill Ann, the Realty bookkeeper. But I'd just as soon Cindi not find out where I spent the afternoon.

I start her chopping onions while I peel ginger. I tell her,

"A lot of men are scared of spices. I've seen guys who've been to war and everything go: *what are those little green specks?*"

"That's Richard." She laughs. And admiring our own bravery, we make Indian chicken hot with cumin, tumeric, asafoetida, put milk and saffron in the rice. I open a jar of lime pickle from the case Charley ordered from New York. Chill some Mexican beer.

We eat in the living room. Cindi hooks up her VCR and runs *Casablanca*. When it's over, she puts on the videotape of her wedding.

"My Dad went all out." She is sitting on the floor in front of the TV, counting her dimes. I'm stretched on the couch cooling my mouth with a Dos Equis. "Like he thought I was Princess Di or something."

After a long shot of the wedding invitation, we see Cindi come out of her house. Palm trees. Bridesmaids. Richard stands at the altar and then Cindi comes down the aisle with her father, who looks about Charley's age. She says, "I was so much cuter then." It's true. There's a bossanova harp soundtrack till we go live for the vows. Richard gulps audibly. Cindi sounds wispy. No indication of how she can yell.

When groups pose in front of the church, Cindi points out her friends. At the reception, she and Richard whirl together. They feed each other cake. She explains that the reception was at a yacht club and for the finale they are to sail into the sunset. Cindi bunches up her wedding dress to step aboard. "Mom kept saying I was going to fall in and ruin the gown. I said, Ma, I'm never going to wear it again, so what?" They sail gracefully, Richard steering. Many drunk people wave. Over the image of the boat going out of sight, pink sky, lavender water, we read "THE END."

"Then we went to a pier where the best man had our car and he took Dad's boat back." Cindi is stacking her dimes into towers. "You know, the month before the wedding was the closest I've ever been with my Mom. She got so excited about the video. It was like she was the director and I was the star."

She looks like she's going to cry so I say, "You're lucky. My mother never liked me that I can remember. Of course, I realize now that she was constantly depressed. She would sit on the sofa and read a magazine, turning the page maybe once in a half hour. She could make the *Ladies Home Journal* last for days. I don't know exactly when she stopped speaking to me. I was fourteen, fifteen. I complained to my Dad and he said,

Your mother's a beautiful woman. You have to be patient, be good. I only realized later how pathetic that was. I would ask her what I had done wrong—Is it kissing Jimmy after skating, Mom? Is it that lipstick I shoplifted? So she knew all my sins and only seemed more gloomy and pissed off. I got through high school staying out all the time—she wouldn't even speak to forbid me. I remember how amazed I was that she showed up at graduation. After the ceremony I raced up to her. And she looked at me and said, Get lost."

"Oh my God," Cindi says. "No wonder you're bitter."

"I don't think I'm bitter. I didn't even get lost right away. I did some time in college, but my Dad didn't have much money and it made more sense to work. And then I just drifted. I slid south. Philadelphia, Baltimore. In D.C. I hooked up with the guy who brought me here. By then I was twenty-six."

"Do you hear from your father?"

"The last few times I wrote I got no answer. I'm pretty sure he's dead."

Cindi gets up and brings me another beer, as if she thinks I merit it.

I've already had too many, but so what. "The strange thing is, I believed she was right, that I was a bad person and she could tell. When I was little, I liked the witches in fairy tales, the evil hags. I knew how they felt. And in my teens I read these historical novels where the only women who did things were the immoral ones. King's mistresses mostly. I must have read twenty books about Anne Boleyn. Do you know she was Henry's mistress for six years? Then he wrecked the Catholic church to marry her and inside of two years he was fooling around with someone else and she wound up beheaded."

"Damn Richard," Cindi says, "where *was* he last night?"

I realize she's fairly drunk too. And glaring.

"Hey, don't look at me. I never even speak to Richard."

"Really? I thought maybe you went to see him this afternoon, to like talk things over."

Was I supposed to do that for her? "No, I had a picnic to go to."

"You know," she says, "you have really nice nail polish."

I laugh.

"No, I mean it. I mean, your toenails and fingernails match and everything."

I look at my nails. "A sign of time on my hands."

Cindi says, "I bet lots of men want to date you and you're

like twenty-seven."

"I'll be thirty in the fall." I get up.

"You see?" she wails. "Why did I get married?"

She follows me to the closet and I hand her sheets and towels. "Well, why did you?"

"I thought Richard was a *man*." She stands hugging a pillow while I make up the couch. "Men, you know what I mean? They carry wallets, they shave, they laugh at things you never get to hear. I wanted one of those."

"Uhhuh. I think it's their shoulders."

"Then you get one and he fusses if the blankets come untucked, but really he can't sleep because he's so worried Charley Yow is going to fire him. Then he sits up all night reading old comic books. Melissa, I forgot my toothbrush. Can I use the extra one in the bathroom?"

"Oh sure. That's the guest toothbrush. Go right ahead." I turn off the air conditioning and open the sliding doors. As I wait for the night breeze, I hear her brushing her teeth with Charley's toothbrush. I wonder how much she's been nosing around. And yet, I kind of like having her here. I must be very drunk.

She comes out in a frilled nightgown and peignoir set like the ones girls wear in vampire movies. She arranges herself on the couch. I say, "You know, I think it must be tough being a man and having to keep up that front of assurance. When a man marries, maybe he's looking for the one person he can trust to let him drop all that, someone he can break down on."

"Someone to throw up all over, you mean."

"Yeah, I guess."

"But if he was out earlier showing off for some other woman, acting like he's so great, it isn't fair." She says "it isn't fair" just like a child.

I turn off the lights and tell her to get some rest.

After an hour I'm still awake and developing the whirlies. I slip into the living room without disturbing Cindi's sleeping hiss and grab the box of comic books. By three a.m. I'm feeling sick from their pace—event event event event. I picture Richard with this ideal of Action, going two months without a sale. The superheroes are streamlined, with frightening thighs. The women look like superheroes with rocket breasts. I prefer the villains, who are characterized by baldness, dwarfishness, stutters, and who are always seeking power they do not naturally possess. In other words, ordinary men.

At seven forty-five I come to in a bed full of superheroes. I've showered before I realize Cindi's gone. With her possessions. She folded the sheets and washed last night's dishes. I drink some orange juice in salute to her on the road to Florida. Richard's comics I pack up and bring to work.

From the sky, the Yow Realty building is a Y. It's true, I've seen it. When Charley takes me up in his plane, he likes to fly out over the malls and buzz his stretch of blue mirrored glass. It was old Mr. Yow's last project and I believe a vision of the utility bills stroked him into retirement. Not a window in it you can open. And yet it comforts me to work here. From inside my office, looking across the parking lot towards Carolina Mall, I get that sense of cool immunity sunglasses give you.

After a couple of hours of drinking coffee and typing thank you notes to everyone who helped to make the golf tournament such a success, I'm starting to feel normal. Then Charley dashes out and comes back leading Richard.

Since his wedding video, Richard has gone downhill. Then he had the big chin and bulgy athleticism of the fraternity success, the guy who is a champ at chugging contests, picking up chicks, and intramural sports. Now he's just a lousy salesman, as miserably uncomfortable as his cheap suit, shapeless and a bad color.

When Charley shuts his door I never catch more than a rumble. After twenty minutes he comes out and dumps an armload of papers on the table at the far end of my office, which is usually reserved for closings. He seats Richard there. "Melissa, this young man is goin to work in here, studyin all the documents on the Rose Briar project. He's goin to figure out who owes who what." This is a terrible punishment. No matter how little a salesman makes, he gets to hang around the lounge waiting for prospects and shooting the breeze, gets to bustle out on calls real or invented.

I say, "Oh, Charley, can I get you to sign these now," and take my sheaf of letters to his office.

He drops into his chair, takes a pen from the desk set trophy his wife had made with the ball from his hole-in-one, and starts signing. He lets out air as if he's been holding his breath. "That boy's got no bid-ness in sales. Know what? He came to work today in a *taxicab*. Ah saw him. And when Ah axe him about it, what's he say? His wife has the car on a trip to the beach. Ah mean, the Realty's been pickin up the lease payments, advance against commission." His signature is a jab. "Hell, he'll never make a commission."

"Then why don't you fire him?" I go around behind Charley and rub his head.

"Ah've known his daddy thirty years and he axed me, bring the boy home, get him out of Florida. Oh that feels good."

"What's wrong with Florida?"

"Oh, you know, Florida, it's just a hot north anymore. Full of drugs and foreign types. Goddamn—oh, hell, Ah'm gettin to sound as bad as my daddy." He bends so I can get at his neck. "We went to see him last night at the nursin home."

Old Mr. Yow seems so legendary that I'm always startled to realize he can be visited. I ask how he is.

"He'll live forever. Beats me though—years of speech therapy and all he can do is cuss. It's strange."

"Why?"

"Mmm, seems to me that as we forget we'd just drift on back to the earliest things we heard, you know—hush hush and there there sugarpiebaby."

"What a lovely idea." I drop a kiss onto his hair. Charley takes my hand and presses it against his cheek. I can feel the pattern of his scar. Old Mr. Yow's mark. "Maybe it's your true self that's left at the end, though." I laugh, "I'm sure to be an old bitch."

"Baby, you're sweeter than you think." He kisses my palm, licks it a little, then sighs, "But today, Ah'm countin on you to make that boy quit."

"Oh, Charley, come on."

He stands up, buttons his jacket. "You can do it. Be mean. If he resigns, his daddy can't blame me." He gives me a kiss. "Ah got a meetin. Zonin."

"Okay," I say, "go zone."

"That's right, honey, be mad. Take it out on the boy."

I trail out after him. Richard has his head down on the table, sleeping or weeping. I can't do it. I flee down the hall to Bookkeeping.

If I have a friend here, it's Jill Ann. I think in a way she's proud of me as a clever piece of bookkeeping, the mistress of the Realty, not a trace of me in any account that Charley's

wife can see. Somewhere in her 40's, Jill Ann is twice divorced.
I find her eating peanut butter crackers and drinking diet soda.
We say "Hey." I take a can of Tab from the fridge and sit on
the antique safe that came from old Mr. Yow's original office.

"You don't look so good this mornin," Jill Ann says. "You
catchin cold? Well, of course. Look at that dress—what's that,
cotton?—that's that kind that's *supposed* to be wrinkledy, isn't
it? And no stockins. I've told you before, a pant suit's the only
thing with all this hoppin in and out of air conditionin." Jill
Ann's red pants suit sets off her country-western blue-black
hair.

"I'm fine. I'm just tired from the weekend."

"Tell me," says Jill Ann. "Drinkin?" I nod. "And then
you go out in that sun? Fries you up. Me and Marco..." And she
is launched on this weekend's adventures with her boyfriend, a
hairdresser somewhat younger than she is, who she met at a
drive-in barbeque place two years ago. The metal of the safe is
numbing my ass, the central air gusts cold, and the pale blue
world beyond the glass seems undersea. Yeah, this is what I
need, to listen to Jill Ann talk and talk...and then she mentions
Richard. "Saturday, bout six o'clock? We saw him at the
Marlin Lounge, you know, at the Holiday House? Marco took
me there to hear the Drifters. Anyway, they have two for one
Happy Hour and ooh baby was he knockin them back. Vodka
tonics. Was he alone? Of course not. When were you born? He
was with this little honey, she had on a cute outfit, I must say.
Pink. Pink high heel sandals..."

I hold the cold soda can against my forehead, thinking of
Cindi, and decide I might as well go make him quit. Though I
don't want to move, I say, "Jill Ann, I better let you get back to
your work."

"Work? You know what I'm doin today? Grant figures for
that park of Mrs. Yow's. Charley Jr. is donatin my time. It's a
write-off."

Her voice is so full of scorn I ask what's wrong with the
park.

"Nothin. That neighborhood's trashy, it can use a park,
though why she wants us to remember a bunch of Yankees
sneakin down here and lootin Major Yow's plantation—" Jill
Ann winks at me. "Well, maybe that does make sense. You
know she wants a statue of Miss Savannah Yow, who put the
family silver down the well? Ooh baby, think of all that
tarnish. No, it's just I don't care for non-profit. I learned this

business from old Mr. Yow—Charley Sr.?—and what he'd of done is built an industrial park, lured down some northern companies, and stole back a few dollars. Then he'd of taken the profit and gone on and built somethin else. Charity is just loss, loss, loss, exceptin the tax benefit. I mean, do you believe somethin's good only if it's done without hope of return?"

"When I was a kid, the nuns said we were supposed to be good for pure love of God. Like the martyrs." I lean back to get that last metallic drop of soda. "But it's true they always fell back on heaven and hell."

"With my first husband—Deighton, the one that was a preacher?—it was all hell. Ooh baby, you should of heard him go on about how those lusts of the flesh were gonna get you burnt up? Of course, me, I was so dumb I thought it was a turn-on."

I smile, yawn, say, "You know, I did this numerology thing and it said I have no compassion. But I guess I knew I wasn't the non-profit type." I aim the empty can at the trash, make the shot.

"Listen, Melissa, are you feeling bad for what you get from Charley Jr.?"

I click my heels against the safe, trying to decide what I do feel. "He could drop me tomorrow and I wouldn't have any claim on him. And he just gives me what he wants to give and can afford to—"

"Lord knows," says Jill Ann.

"—while he wants me. It seems honest to me. While a wife expects a whole future for love given now, or ten years back—"

"Tell me," she says. "In my experience marriage is just the rashest speculation there is. It's like buyin land from the prospectus full of promises and pretty pictures."

"Well, I shouldn't talk, I've never done it." I shiver.

"There, you see? You go tell Charley you're ill. And go shoppin. Get you a pants suit. Scoot now, I got to donate my day." She shakes her dark hair. "Loss, loss, loss."

Richard appears to be working. I start an Intent to Purchase, botch it, wrench it out of the machine. Corrections look like hell on parchment paper. Next try, I mess up "Herewith." I clap my hands to settle them down. Shake them. It's no use. I have to get rid of Richard.

I go over to his table. He has the Rose Briar plats spread out, but all he's doing is staring at a sheet of paper headed THE REALTOR'S PHILOSOPHY.

I read over his shoulder:

1. REALTY PLUS I = REALITY.

I bite the inside of my cheek.

2. AT THE END OF THE DAYS OF THE TRULY GREAT LEADER, THE PEOPLE WILL SAY ABOUT HIM, WE DID IT OURSELVES. LAO TZU.

I ask what Lao Tzu is.

Richard has the slow serene speech of someone who hasn't slept for a long time. "He was a Chinese. Way back before Christ. He wrote the first manual on salesmanship. He means. You have to let folks sell themselves. It's like—" he waves his arm, "ju jitsu. Just lay back and let them lean on out until they fall—" he sketches a languid dive, "of their own weight. Oh. I know it sounds easy. But no. You can't help it, you want, you press, and fshshsht—they're gone." He sighs, stretches. "I study these every mornin. They're from my real estate course last fall." He tilts the paper for me to read, proud of his difficult precepts.

3. ASK WHY NOT.

I say, "Now there's a good one, Richard. Ask why not. Why not get your tail in gear, quit this joint, and go after your wife."

He grabs my wrist. "I don't know where she is. Nobody knows where she is. Hospitals, state troopers. Do you know where she is?"

And I'm explaining how she's homesick and gone back to Florida, how she's hurt but if he'll just apologize and make the big gesture, like moving back there, everything can be okay, I'm way into my pitch when here's Cindi in the doorway, screeching, "I knew it, Richard, you bastard—" But it's me she jumps.

It's been a long long time since I was in a girlfight. I cover my face with my hands and hunch. She's all over me in a series of sharpnesses: kicks, scratches, bites. I keep thinking Richard will pull her off, but he doesn't, and then she yanks my hair, which I can't stand, so I uncover and take a slice across my cheek before I grab her arms. I'm taller than she is and in better shape. I pin her down on the table. She tries to spit up into my face but it falls back on her and she starts to cry.

"He's mine," she whimpers.   "Give him back give him back."

"Oh hell."   I look at Richard, who's over in the corner, laying back like the truly great leader.

And Cindi is looking at him too, sobbing, "Mine.   Mine mine mine *mine*."

I'm holding her down, but it's more like a hug.   "Hush now, hush," I say.   "Calm down and tell me what happened.   I thought you were driving home."

She sniffs, gulps.   "I tried, but at the first fill-up I felt so stupid, counting out all those dimes, and I thought, oh no, you won't get rid of me like this."   She squints at me.   "I knew what you were up to."

Looking at her, I feel like crying too.

"Oh," I say, "what made you suspicious?"

"I saw you one time in the winter at a," she takes a three gasp breath, "Realty party.   You had on a black silk strapless dress.   And so, when Richard didn't come home, I thought, who's worth going after around here?"

"Flattering."

"I know you have it all over me, with your weird spices and your exercise machines—"

"What'd you do, go through all the closets?"

She nods.

"So, you hung around, you ate my dinner, you stayed over, thinking all the time—"

New big tears appear.   God, she's a mess.   "I kept expecting Richard.   And then I thought, if you like saw the wedding, you'd understand and give him back to meeee."   Her "me" goes off like a siren.

"Okay," I say.   "You want him, you can have him."

I feel her tense.   "It's true then?"

"It wasn't what you think," I say.   "Right, Richard?"

He blinks.

"Just a few drinks in the Marlin Lounge, a few laughs, right Richard?"

"Yes," he says.   "That's right.   That's all it was.   Too much vodka, Cindi, that's all, I swear."

She asks me, "What about the toothbrush, the razor, what about," she sniffs, "the styptic pencil?"

"No, no, Richard didn't get that far.   That's somebody else."

She nods.   "You're wicked.   You told me so yourself."

"That's right," I say, "that's right.   Now hush."   She's completely limp and when I let go she just curls into herself on the table. Under her drippy nose I see a photo of the Rose Briar model home. I pull it out and smooth it. Yesterday I was so happy there.

Richard brings over tissues from my desk and wipes her face. As I back off he moves in, puts his arms around her. She says, "Richard, she doesn't love you like I do."

He says he knows that.

They murmur. I sit at my desk, take out a mirror, and inspect the damages. My scratch is red, angled like warpaint. "Richard," I say, "I have your comics here."

He jumps up.

"Don't touch her," Cindi says.

"No, I won't," he says. He leans and I slide the carton towards him, the two of us cautious as a Berlin prisoner exchange. Just as he snags it, Charley comes in, all lineny and cool.

"What's happenin here?" he asks lazily.

Richard announces that for personal reasons he must regretfully resign. He and his wife wish to live in Florida.

"Well, Ah'm sorry to hear it, son."

"I owe you money, sir, I know, but I can sell some things," Richard offers the carton, "and pay you back."

"Ah'll trust you for it." They shake hands. Cindi looks soothed by male ritual. Richard says goodbye to me. She doesn't. As they leave her look reminds me of my mother.

Charley hugs me tight, tight. "Melissa, you're a pistol." He touches my scratch. "What's this?"

"Oh, guess I'd gotten out of practice on my meanness." I press my cheek against his. "Now we match."

"Baby, Ah'll make it up to you," he says.. "What would you like?"

I shake my head.

"Come on. Axe me. Ah'll give you anythin you want."

"Anything?"   I wind my arms around his neck and whisper, "anything at all?"

I watch his face get serious as he thinks: Mall, airplane, house, daughter, wife.   "Yes," he says, "anythin Ah got. Everythin Ah have."

The seats of the convertible burn. I have to use bunches of my skirt to touch the steering wheel. I drive though flowered streets, punch radio buttons till the Drifters sing. We pass grand magnolias, Yow "FOR SALE" signs, sprinklers kissing lawns. Beside me Charley grins. I reach to touch one golden eyebrow. It couldn't have been mercy, no, must have been greed that made me say, "I'll take the afternoon."

WAMPUM

Jeannie has learned to keep her treasures with her at all times. Otherwise her mother throws them out. So now in one jacket pocket she carries the dead snake that she is planning to skin to make an Indian headband, and in the other her popbead necklace, her pair of blue sunglasses, the tiny bottle of perfume her father gave her that her mother says stinks, and her glass collection. She presses her arms to her sides to hold everything in and squeezes through the break in the grammar school fence. She chases the others. They are going home the Avenue way, which is forbidden.

First they must run by the A & P where somebody's mother might see them, but then they can go collecting past the Pontiac dealer with the big chief out front, past the carpet store where sometimes perfect doll's rugs are stacked by the garbage, past the Wash-a-Rama car wash and Jack's Tavern and the Hi-Lo sheet music store. From the bridge over the brook it's not far to the corner where Maxie's sells candy bars and comic books and this spring has wax fangs with cherry syrup in them.

There's honking traffic and men get into fistfights at Jack's Tavern, but only on the Avenue can you find the rarest colors of broken glass. Here, at night, tossed out of cars and brushed out of stores, accumulate gorgeous pieces of the world.

Other kids trade, especially the red and the very rare purple glass, but Jeannie only likes the pieces she finds herself. She takes out the wavery oval with the bubbles in it, which she believes is ancient and came from the sea. She looks up through it and the sky turns green. Pale blue. Sea green.

She almost passes Sara Lowenthal and Pepper Elliot. They are standing knee to knee, close to the pricker bushes by the Hi-Lo music store.

"That's stealing," Sara says. "You want to steal it but I found it first and you know it."

Pepper asks, "How come my foot is on it then?" His face, pug nosed and clever, mocks her.

"My foot too." And they tug at a piece of paper with their shoes, so it looks like it'll get torn.

"What is it?" Jeannie asks Pepper because Sara is crying.

"Treasure," he says.

"My treasure," Sara wails.

"You pick it up, Jeannie," says Pepper. "Everybody knows you didn't find it."

Jeannie squats and they take their feet away. It's money. She picks some mud off it. It's a hundred dollar bill. Ben Franklin is on it, his face damp and spotted.

"I found it. I *found* it. You're a cheat," Sara mourns as they walk along. Jeannie has handed the bill over to Pepper, who is cleaning and smoothing it against his shirt. One corner got torn but Pepper says it is still worth one hundred dollars.

"I'm wealthy," he says. "I'm rich." He skips ahead and says he's going to spend it all at Maxie's, going to buy Maxie's whole supply of Bonomo Banana Turkish Taffee.

When Sara cries her chin looks long and you notice that her mother cut her bangs too short. Jeannie says, "You can't spend it all, Pepper. You found it together and you'll have to split it."

To her this seems fair, but Sara and Pepper won't split. They turn down their street, still fighting.

When they get to Sara's driveway, Pepper says he is going to take the bill home and put it in his bank that only he knows how to open.

Sara says she will tell her mother and her mother will call the police because Pepper is a robber.

Pepper says, "I'm rubber, you're glue, everything you say bounces off me and sticks to you," but Jeannie can tell he is bothered.

He runs off toward his house and Sara goes sobbing up her driveway. Jeannie heads home.

The hardest part each day is getting her collection in and out of the house. This morning her mother told her not to wear her jacket, but she waited till her parents were arguing and sneaked by. Now she folds her jacket over her arm so nothing will fall out.

Her mother is working out front in the rock garden. When Jeannie was little the whole slope was honeysuckle and all the kids came over on nice May days like this and slid down, the juice from the honeysuckle making each slide slipperier. But Jeannie's mother called the kids "a howling tribe" and tore out "that mess" and now instead they have rocks and flowers in patches like a quilt.

Jeannie's mother weeds bent over in her old Bermuda shorts. Jeannie gets partway up the driveway before she says, "You took your time. Drew's home already." Drew never beats her home, he's only in first grade. Her mother straightens up, wiping her forehead with her wrist. "It's broiling." Jeannie nods. "Go in the front," her mother says, "I've opened up the porch."

As she walks up the steps, Jeannie can feel her mother looking at her jacket. So she says, "Sara Lowenthal and Pepper Elliot found some money today," and then remembers it was on the Avenue.

But all her mother says is "Oh?" and "Wipe your feet," so Jeannie gets inside. On the porch the grass rug is half unrolled and in the living room the green wicker chairs, down from the attic, wait to be set out. Her mother must have decided it's summer. When the seasons change, her mother always changes everything.

Up in her room, she switches from her pleated skirt to dungarees. She can put her glass into the pockets. And the sunglasses and necklace and perfume she hides in the hatbox in her closet inside her black velveteen beret. But the snake? It won't be safe in her dresser and when she crawls under the bed and tries to lay it along the little shelf under the springs it is too wide and falls down. Finally she pulls the Marjorie Maynard books out of her bookcase and arranges the snake behind them. The books are old ones of her grandmother's, about a family who all the time write the daughter poems like, "Marjorie Parjorie Mopsy the Minx, Why does Marjorie always cut jinx?" "Cut jinx" is their word for get in trouble and that's what happens in every book, Marjorie gets in trouble by falling off a roof or drinking poison by mistake and then she gets scolded but forgiven in poems from everybody.

Her mother comes upstairs and calls from the bathroom, "Why are you inside? It's a beautiful day."

"I'm reading." Meanwhile Jeannie is sliding the last book perfectly into line. Not even her mother could suspect.

"Well, go play with your brother. Go outside and blow the stink off yourself."

This is her mother's favorite thing to say to kick them out of the house. Jeannie shuts the closet door, checks her bookcase, and leaves.

Their backyard has a two swing swingset, a big pine tree, and a fireplace where Drew is using his metal shovel to chop pine needles.

Jeannie sits on the higher swing. "Whatcha doing?"

"Making fertilizer. To sell people for their gardens."

Drew brushes the chopped needles into a paper bag, then gathers another handful. He sprinkles them with salt and pepper from the kitchen shakers. He always has some business going, like when he took a bottle of her mother's perfume and put it in an ice cube tray in the freezer. He was planning to sell it to ladies as solid cologne only it got used when her father made her mother a highball to make up after a fight. Her father says Drew is a schemer. He cheats at cards and he won't do anything unless you bribe him. Jeannie doesn't think he's very smart. Like once he bought candy bars at Maxie's and buried them under the roots of the pine tree so of course they were all full of ants when he dug them up. And she can always fool him into choosing the smallest cookie by the way she stacks them.

Now Drew spits into the paper bag three times and says, "Ready for my sales trip." He pulls the wagon out of the garage and it's loaded with a dozen lunch bags. He wheels down the driveway. In the sunshine his crewcut is silver and he's singing his favorite, "Great green gobs of greasy grimey gopher guts..." Jeannie often thinks he's cute when he doesn't know she can see him.

It's such a beautiful day. Jeannie leans way back in her swing and pumps. Soon she's going as high as the swingset allows, at the top her sneakers almost touching pine branches, on the downswing her braids brushing the ground. She closes her eyes to get dizzier and dares herself to jump on the next swing — no, the next — and lands with a tumble and rolls over and over in the pine needles. She opens her eyes and upside down and backwards sees Sara Lowenthal at the back fence.

"I thought you were my best friend," Sara says.

Jeannie crosses the whirling yard. "I still am."

"You want to come over?" Sara still looks sad but not as terrible as before. So Jeannie jumps the low wire fence and follows her.

Lowenthals have the best yard in the neighborhood. It runs the whole way from their house to Jeannie's. The tumbledown shed, so Sara said, was once a station of the Underground Railroad in the Civil War and the house, Sara said, used to be the mansion of the people who owned the town.

They go into the kitchen and sit at the wooden table. Sara brings ice tea. Lowenthals have ice tea with grape juice all year round. Jeannie doesn't really like it but it's what you drink at their house. Sara told her once that they bought their house when they were rich but then her father was cheated so they couldn't afford new furniture. But then another time she said that when her parents came to America they bought the house because it was like their home in Hungary and all the furniture came from their ancestors. Jeannie knows Sara doesn't always tell the truth but it doesn't seem to matter. Sara is always sadder than Jeannie. Her parents don't fight like Jeannie's, but they are very old, like grandparents.

Now Sara says, "You saw me find that money."

"Sara, I wan't looking. Did you find it first?"

Sara's chin gets long. "I thought we were best friends."

"We are." Jeannie drinks her ice tea with grape juice.

About a month ago was when Sara told her that although everyone at school called her a crybaby, really she couldn't help it. "The doctor says I have over active tear ducks," she said. "That's the place where the water comes out and mine, the doctor said, are just like a leaky faucet you can't turn off." So Sara wasn't as much of a crybaby as everyone thought and Jeannie became her best friend.

Sara says, "Let's watch TV," and they go down the hall to the living room. Sara's sister Bunny, who is in high school, is there with her friend watching American Bandstand and drinking ice tea with grape juice. Sara says, "We want to dance," and Bunny says, "Okay, doll, but you'll have to be boys," and Sara whispers, "It's okay, the boys do the same thing," but Jeannie already knows that. At Sara's mostly they watch American Bandstand and dance. They do the Stroll and Bunny taught them the Bunny Hop.

The big thing now, though, is the Twist. Dick Clark talks, then the music starts and the kids on television and Bunny and her friend and Sara and Jeannie do the Twist, squishing one foot back and forth. Jeannie can get real low like Bunny, who makes her skirts swirl around and whirl up just like the girls on television. Mrs. Lowenthal comes in and says something they can't hear over the music. Then Bunny grabs her hand and Mrs. Lowenthal starts dancing too although she makes it look more like square dancing and they all Twist until the commercial when they collapse on the couch. Mrs. Lowenthal laughs, then looks very sad.

"Voice lessons this afternoon," she says. Bunny groans and goes upstairs with her friend. Sara and Jeannie wait outside. Sara takes lots of lessons: voice and piano and flute and Hebrew and ballet. Sara has promised to teach Jeannie to sing like her; her voice is very even as it goes from word to word and she knows harmony, which is just like Sara, melancholy, so Jeannie is sure she'll never get it. They sit on the stone bench in the front yard singing Michael Rowed the Boat Ashore and Sara makes the Alleluia's heartbreaking.

"I found that hundred dollars," Sara says. "I was walking along looking for more of that purple glass and I saw the money first."

Jeannie starts humming Come On Baby, Let's Do The Twist, but Sara is crying, "You believe me don't you?"

And Jeannie has to say, "I believe you."

Mrs. Lowenthal and Bunny come out and get in the car with Sara and pull down the driveway.

Jeannie walks down with Bunny's friend, who says, "I'm going up to the Avenue to see what I can find. Maybe a diamond ring."

As Jeannie walks down the block past her own house, she is achy in her stomach for having told Sara she believes her. She decides to find Pepper.

Elliots live at the end of the street. Once Mrs. Elliot and her mother were best friends and babysat for each other and gave her and Pepper baths together. Jeannie can't remember that, even when she tries hard with her eyes squeezed. Though she doesn't think of Pepper as one of the boys who you like or who like you and shove you down on the playground to show it. Pepper is friendly like a dog, waggy and smart. He loves to give wrong answers, like "distraction" for "subtraction," and that's how he got his name, because he said the four tastes were sour, sweet, salt, and pepper. Before that his name was Douglas.

Pepper opens the door when she rings the bell. "I can't go out," he says. "I'm being punished."

Jeannie asks how come.

"When I showed Mom the hundred dollar bill she said I must have stolen it. She never believes me. So I'm being punished for going on the Avenue and maybe stealing. She took the money, too, till my dad comes home and straightens things out."

That's why Pepper's mother and hers had been friends, probably, because they were both strict. But then Jeannie's father told off Mrs. Elliot one time and they stopped.

They stand in the living room, where the Venetian blinds are down. There are lilacs in a bowl. Jeannie feels a little frightened, as always at Elliots'.

"What do you want to do?" Pepper asks.

"We could work on your collections."

"I'm tired of my collections."

"We could go up to the attic." That's where Pepper's father hides his *Playboy* magazines. One winter they put together a puzzle they found there and later Pepper got that puzzle for Christmas, so they knew there was no Santa. They were first in their class.

"I know," Pepper says, "we can look at the encyclopedia." So they go up to Mr. Elliot's study and sit on the floor by the bookcase. They look up diseases, to see the pictures. Pepper likes the vitamin deficiencies, like scurvy and pellegra, but Jeannie prefers rare diseases. She always looks at the elephantiasis picture. Sometimes she can stand to look at the illustration for leprosy but sometimes she can't.

Pepper gets them some Fig Newtons and they start to follow the See Also's. "Look up rigor mortis," he says.

She does. "No picture."

Pepper says, "Splitting the money with Sara isn't fair. Mom will make me but it isn't fair. I found it." He turns the encyclopedia pages in big clumps.

Jeannie believes him. It just isn't likely that Sara saw the money — she's much slower at finding things and then she always claims she saw them first. So Jeannie says, "I'm sure you found it."

"Thanks. But my mom will never believe me." He stands up. "I have a present for you, come on."

He leads her into his parents' bedroom. It's fancier than her parents' room and has twin beds and twin dressers, like people on television. Pepper feels around in the wastebasket and pulls out a gold lipstick. "She swore," he says, "and threw it out." They examine the case. The thing that twists the color up is broken, so the only way to get the lipstick is to hold it upside down. The color is beautiful. Summer Roses it says on the bottom.

Pepper hands her the lipstick and she thanks him politely.

Jeannie holds the lipstick upside down and, tilting her head back, rubs it on her lips. Then she takes a tissue and smacks her mouth against it like her mother does.

Someone is coming up the stairs. Pepper grabs her hand and pulls her into the closet and swings the door shut after them. Something furry brushes her face. They squeeze behind his father's suits. It's hard to find a place to stand among the shoes. Everything smells like leather and mothballs. She holds her breath. She hears the whistle of air through Pepper's nose and outside the clonks of his mother kicking off her shoes. The door opens and Jeannie can see the edge of Mrs. Elliot's slip, her legs in stockings as she throws her loafers in and takes out a pair of high heels. Hangers zing back and forth across the pole. "Hell," says Mrs. Elliot. She takes something out and shuts the door. Then they don't hear anything. They stand there so long Jeannie can see patterns in the darkness. She is holding Pepper's hand. "Is she gone?" Jeannie breathes and Pepper kisses her, his lips wet like he just licked them, and she is so surprised she doesn't have time to purse up her lips like you're supposed to, so he sort of kisses her tooth. Then he says, "Don't tell," and opens the door and they're out.

She is still surprised while she follows him downstairs and onto the front step. He has a mark of lipstick on his mouth. When she tells him he takes a leaf and wipes it off. He says, "I'm not supposed to be outside."

"I'll go home now. It's probably five."

Pepper grins. "My dad will be home. He'll get me my money."

She walks home slowly, every so often squeezing her eyes shut to remember the kiss but mostly she gets the smell of shoes. She has the lipstick in her pocket.

She sits on her front steps. Soon her father will be home. She decides to tell him about the money and how she has told Sara and Pepper that she believes each of them. Her father is always easier on her than her mother. He's a big believer in confession, her mother says.

Her mother is behind her on the porch, laying down the rug with grunts and sighs. But it isn't any use to try and help. Her mother does everything herself.

Her father comes up the driveway in his blue Chevy and stops short. When he gets out of the car he has his jacket off and his tie undone already. He gets up the slate steps in two strides.

"Home so soon?" her mother says.

"Why the hell not?" Her father is looking in through the screen porch door.

"Jack's will go out of business. Did you use up your allowance already?"

"Now isn't that silly," he says to Jeannie. "Your old man with an allowance. Twelve dollars a week for lunches and shoeshines and all the needs of life."

That was the big fight last week, her father's allowance, because he lost a lot of money on a bet.

"But your old man is pretty clever."

Jeannie hears her mother tug something heavy onto the porch.

"Your old man," he raises his voice, "doubled his allowance this week."

"Oh, Gene," her mother says.

He passes Jeannie and says, "Well, let me give you a hand, Margaret," and Jeannie twists around to see him toss his jacket and tie into the living room. Her mother sighs and goes in and picks them up and puts them in the closet while her father lifts the porch chairs lightly over the sill and arranges them the way they are arranged every summer. Then he comes back out and sits beside her on the steps. Jeannie sniffs, pretending she likes the rock garden but really examining her father's smells. He always has a warm and complicated scent that she cannot identify.

"Where's your brother, slippery Pierre?"

"Out someplace."

"Lucky him. You want to go someplace? Margaret," he calls inside, "I'm taking Jeannie for a walk. Work up our appetites for — what are we having?"

She comes out onto the porch. "It's lamb chops."

"Well, we'll definitely be back for lamb chops," he says. "Won't we?"

Her mother says, "Dinner's at six. They'll be burnt by six-fifteen."

"Lay off, Margaret," says her father.

Her room whirls round and round and round. When she sits up it spins more slowly and it's almost still when she stands. But she doesn't want to stand. She wants to lie down. She takes out a book to get calm but all the words sink into the page and split into other words and she can't make any sense of them. She can't read. She's lost the trick of it. She'll be sent back to first grade. She'll be stupider than Drew. She starts crying only she wants to lie down to cry but when she does the room whirls. She leans, standing up, against her bed.

When they went for a walk she told her father about the money and he took her up to the Avenue so she could show him the exact spot and then he said they were right by Jack's, why not stop in and talk it over?

A lot of cars were parked between the Hi-Lo music store and Jack's Tavern. One man had a litter of beagle puppies in a box in his back seat. Her father introduced her to him and another man and then inside she met Jack himself, who stood behind the bar. Her father said, "This is my kid Jeannie. Today she and her buddies found a hundred dollar bill."

"No Daddy, Pepper and Sara found it."

"Still, it's lucky." He winked at the bartender. "I'll have a shot and a chaser and the young lady will have a Manhattan." That's what her father called Cokes with maraschino cherries in them, Manhattans.

She got her Coke in a highball glass. She liked the way it looked in the bar, deeply red and glamorous. Her father clinked his glass against hers before they drank. She always saved the cherry for last.

She could see herself in the mirror straight ahead, between the pyramids of bottles. It seemed to her her lips were still red with lipstick, so she looked grown up. Above the mirror were pictures of ladies, all smiling, with numbers on them.

She asked her father who they were.

He said they were the Miss Rheingold contestants and that she could vote for Miss Rheingold if she wanted. He told Jack to bring her a few ballots and he gave her a pile of them and a short pencil. She started marking all the ballots for number six, who was the only blond one.

"Keep an eye on her for a minute," her father said. "I'm going next door."

"Where?" she asked as he got off the stool.

"I'm just going to the Hi-Lo. Going to buy a few good numbers." And he and the bartender laughed.

After she finished the ballots, Jack put them in a box beside the cash register and it began to seem like a long time. The bottles looked pretty, doubled in the mirror. The glass was mostly clear or brown or green.

A man sat down next to her while she was chewing the maraschino cherry.

"What are you drinking, kid?" he asked.

"Manhattan Coke."

"Manhattan Coke for her and a Manhattan for me," the man said to Jack. "Who's she?"

"Gene Quinn's kid," said Jack. "He's next door."

"Ah," said the man. He had blond hair in the mirror. Jeannie thought it was more polite to look at him in the mirror.

"Come here often?" he said and then laughed.

"No."

The man looked at her in the mirror.

"Do you like to play the jukebox?" he asked. She shrugged. He pulled change out of his pocket and picked out a quarter. Her drink came and she gulped it. "You get three choices." He went over to the blue and silver jukebox at the end of the bar. "What do you want to hear?"

Jeannie shrugged.

"Come on," he said. "Anything you like."

"Let's Twist Again Like We Did Last Summer," she said. "And Let's Do The Twist and The Peppermint Twist."

The man laughed. "You can't Twist."

"I can too."

"We'll see," he said. She slid down from the stool to watch him punch in the songs. A claw hunted back and forth across the records.

She said, "I want my drink," and the man handed her her soda but it was finished. She ate the cherry and asked for another. "Here," said the man, "you can finish mine." She drank his drink and when she said it tasted funny he said it must have been a rotten cherry.

Then her song came on and she did the Twist and so did the man and some other people. A lady gave her a drink like lemonade and everyone laughed a lot and Twisted and she did the best Twisting she'd ever done, better than Bunny Lowenthal.

Then her father came and got her. He walked fast going home and when they got there he said, "Don't tell," and held her hand going into the dining room. Her mother and Drew were sitting there with food on the table but they hadn't filled their plates yet. And she didn't tell but when she tried to spoon up the mint jelly she dropped a big blob of it on the tablecloth and laughed and her mother said, "Oh my God, Gene," and sent her upstairs.

Now she goes into the bathroom, thinking maybe she'll be sick, but all she gets are burps. Her mother calls her from downstairs. She is only a little dizzy going down the steps. Everyone is on the front porch: her mother and Drew, Mr. and Mrs. Lowenthal with Sara, Mrs. Elliot in a beautiful emerald green dress and Mr. Elliot and Pepper, but not her father. They are all arguing. Her mother pulls Jeannie in between her knees so she is almost sitting on her lap. She undoes one of Jeannie's braids. All the time they talk her mother is rebraiding her hair, very gently, not yanking like she does in the morning.

"He's a bully," Mrs. Lowenthal says. "We know all about bullies. A little girl finds some money and the bully steps on it and takes it away."

"Did you steal from her?" Mrs. Elliot asks Pepper.

"No. I found it first."

"Robber," says Sara. "Bully."

"Ask Jeannie," says Pepper.

"You ask Jeannie," Sara shouts. "She was with me. She saw me find it. You weren't even around."

Jeannie shuts her eyes. She can feel her mother's fingers softly curling through her hair and the big cool bunches of her mother's skirt like a bed. She wishes she were in bed, under the covers.

"Did you see?" her mother asks her.

"I told Daddy."

"He went back out."

"There were together," she says. "I didn't see who found it first."

"Liar," Sara shouts.

Pepper says, "Jeannie, it was mine."

Jeannie's mother says, "It was somebody else's, but I guess there's no point in trying to find out who dropped it there. You'll have to split it." Then they argue about who will get the actual bill. The Lowenthals win. Mr. Elliot hands them the hundred and Mr. Lowenthal searches his wallet and pockets and Mrs. Lowenthal's purse and finally writes Mr. Elliot a check. All the time Pepper and Sara are making faces at her. Then they go away.

"How do you feel?" her mother asks.

She hasn't even yelled at her for being on the Avenue. Jeannie lies, "Okay."

Her mother stands at the screen door looking out. She is pretty in her pale dress. "It's still light. Why don't you go outside and play?"

"I don't want to."

Her mother suddenly turns into her regular self. "Get some fresh air and sober up," she says. "Blow the stink off yourself." She watches Jeannie go down the steps.

Jeannie runs to the back, hoping to sneak back into the house, but Pepper and Sara are waiting. She knew they would be. They grab her arms and march her into Sara's yard. They drag her into the shed. Pepper pinches her arms and shoves her into the corner.

"I'll give you the lipstick back," she says.

"What do I want with a lipstick? You're a liar," he whispers, "and if you try and tell anybody I kissed you they won't believe you because I'm going to tell everyone you're a liar and I hate you."

Sara brings over an old iron gate. They block her in with it and pile junk against it.

"Come on, Sara, we're still friends. Let me out."

"Do you hear something?" Sara asks Pepper.

He says, "Must be a rat." They chant "Jeannie the rat, the lying lying rat" to the Felix the Cat song.

Then Pepper pulls Sara's hair. "You owe me fifty dollars and I'm going to get it from you if it takes me the rest of my life," he says. Sara runs away crying and he chases her.

Jeannie can see the sky through a hole in the roof. It's

almost dark enough for stars. She thinks she could break out if she wasn't so tired. Too tired to scream. Anyway no one will hear her. No one cares. No one else sees things the way she sees them. Like a stripey shell under the ocean, just for this one instant of vacation it's here where you are, and as you grab a wave knocks you down and you come up spitting water and laughing because you rescued it. Or the curtains swelling in the morning when you can smell pancakes and you think about your brain thinking and then when you get up there's one tiny pancake, like the child of the big ones. No one else feels like that. Everybody just wants money. Moolah, her father calls it, bananas, sawbucks, fins. It makes her tired. She tries to settle in her corner so she can sleep. When she leans back she can see, worn and barely shiny, the moon like an old old coin.

"*Go*pher guts, little *bird*ies' bloody feet, mutil*a*ted monkey meat — "

"Drew," she hollers. "Drew, Drew, I'm captured. It's Jeannie."

He calls her and then she sees him in the shed.

"Get me out."

"What'll you give me?" he says.

She stands up. "I'll give you a dollar."

"Okay, throw it to me."

"I don't have it with me. Come on, Drew, it's in my bank. You can have it as soon as we're home."

Drew comes near the gate and looks in. "No you won't, Jeannie. You always trick me."

"Oh." She can tell him to go home and get her mother, but he'll want payment for that too. In her pockets she has ony her lipstick and her glass collection.

"Well," she sighs, "I guess — I don't want to give it up — but I guess I'll have to give you my — wampum."

"Huh?"

"Wampum. It's Indian money. Don't you know anything. It's like jewels, not old paper. Sara told me today she'd give me anything for just one of these." She holds her glass pieces out and shakes them. "It's like emeralds and diamonds."

"Diamonds?"

"Wampum." She rolls the word as richly as possible. "Wammpumm. Wammm Pummm."

"Okay," says Drew. "But I want all of them. Toss them over."

"No sir. How do I know you won't take them and leave

me?"

"Oh." He sounds impressed. "Okay. You give me one and I'll open it a little and then you give me the rest while you get out."

So Jeannie hands over her collection gradually and soon she's free.

She leaves Drew in their backyard, looking for someplace to bury his treasure. She doesn't mind losing it; it's just bits of the bottles from Jack's bar.

She moves quietly through the living room. Her parents are on the front porch, sitting in the wicker chairs, silent. She can't tell if this is before the fight or after.

Up in her room, the hatbox with the black velveteen beret is gone. In its place is the white one that holds her straw hat with the blue flowers. Her mother has put the other away for the summer. She knows she cannot ask for it. Perhaps in the fall it will come back with her sunglasses and popbeads and perfume still inside.

She puts on her pajamas. The snake is still in its hiding place. She lifts it out and gets into bed with her book and her snake and her lipstick. She opens *Marjorie's Vacation*. She can read it okay now but she doesn't really want to, it's such a baby book. She holds the lipstick upside down and colors her lips Summer Rose. She remembers Pepper kissing her tooth and that's true no matter what he says. She turns off the light and lies down. Carefully, she places the snake across her forehead. It's beginning to feel papery and it smells. Soon the skin will come off and she'll have her headband. She closes her eyes, planning how she'll be an Indian, wild, brave, and resourceful.

MOON WALK

She walks in the freak light of a sunshower: a tall girl with bright hair, blond or maybe red, down past her shoulders. Her india print dress is short. She wears sandals and carries a heavy shoulder bag, and Bobby knows before he pulls over that she will have wire-rim glasses. As she turns, he sees the hippie flower painted on her thigh, but still he thinks she is a studious girl, shy. She peers into the car. Yes, Timmie Moore.

So he recognized her, though she has changed.

What was she doing? Just walking around.

What was he doing? Just driving. Come on.

Timmie tells him, as they continue along Prospect, that she was heading for the lookout point at Eagle Rock. At her house, as at his, they are watching the moon landing on TV. Her dad has friends over. She helped set the couch up on cinderblocks with chairs down front, two tiers, "Just like for football," she says, "Us versus the Commies." She stayed long enough to lay out a New Jersey buffet: capicola and provolone, kielbassi and tongue, hard rolls, baked beans, beefsteak tomatoes and blueberry pie. Then she took off. "I seized some beer," she says, digging through her bag and bringing out a can. She taps the top, then holds it out the window, kneels out the window to swig off the foam. Bobby glimpses the long backs of her thighs, a blue edge of panty, then she sits again and passes the beer.

He turns down Mt. Pleasant. Here it's misty but they can still see, as they go down the hill, the church steeples of Orange, East Orange, and, hanging beyond them, the New York skyline.

He notices her voice — husky, sardonic when she uses words like "seized" — and realizes he hasn't talked to her since they were fifteen. She's still tall, he thinks, then almost laughs — had he expected her to shrink? But she's very tall, a good 5'10", almost as tall as him. On the bridge of her nose he sees a place — glazed, scaly — where the skin has peeled and peeled again. The painting on her thigh is a butterfly, done in inks, orange and hot pink.

"I couldn't stand it," she is saying.   "They're there watching *cartoons!*   Little rockets with little men in them creeping across the screen. Just drawings. And the announcer, you know, gets all breathless —" She gets all breathless: "And if   this retrorocket   *doesn't fire*   or if it should EXPLODE!   they'll be stuck   Out There   Outcasts   in Endless   Space. You know they just love it. Outcasstsssss in Endlesssss Spacccce. What crap! I couldn't stand it."

He agrees, he couldn't stand it either. But since they were all staying in at his house he'd been allowed the car.

She touches the Chevy insignia on the glovebox. "What happened to your car? The Mustang?"

Sold.

They are at the bottom of the hill now, West Orange. They drive past Edison's laboratories, ivy-darkened buildings where they went on tour as kids. There are no other cars on the road. The whole state, she says, the whole nation, looking in their TV screens like magic mirrors. In Orange, he turns back up the hill. As they approach the entrance to Eagle Rock, Bobby thinks of swinging in — it's where she had been aiming and they could park at the lookout with the view to themselves — but he has let it pass, he isn't sure why. In any case: "I should get gas," he says. "We'll go by Nello's place."

Timmie sits silent, shares the beer, and watches the trees shiver under invisible rain. She has chattered every surface thought away and has only her amazement: *Bobby Giancaspro* stopped for her. *Bobby Giancaspro.* Now, everything lines up to this moment. Yesterday, when she went into the city, her college friends lazed in the druggy sunshine, listened to musicians improvise, but she could sit still only while a runaway girl covered in designs painted her leg for a dollar. Then she raced through street boutiques until she found this dress, its bell sleeves falling longer than the skirt. Today, her mother was busy, so only when she reached to brush back Timmie's hair as she slipped out the door did she notice: "Where'd this rag come from?" Timmie made it to the yard before she said, "What's that thing on your leg?" Timmie laughed. Her mother was afraid; how great; it proved that she had changed. At the beginning of the summer her mother had said, "You're not a virgin, are you?" And Timmie answered no, though she wasn't exactly sure if she was a virgin or not; it had been that kind of freshman year. Today she blew a kiss, said "Don't worry I'll come home," and ran down the driveway almost falling as she had when she was a child.

They swing into Nello's father's Esso station, ringing the bell as they go over the hose, but no one comes out. Bobby tosses the beer can into the trash bucket, hollers, then starts to fill the tank himself. She looks at him in the rear view mirror. In blue jeans, a black t-shirt shrunk too tight at the shoulders, short at the waist: *Bobby Giancaspro.*

He had had the grace which in adolescence is one's whole character; he grew smoothly, his voice slid low, his beard appeared. In ninth grade she sat behind him in World History, memorizing the tips of dark hair on the nape of his neck. From his right in Math I she learned the intersection of his forehead and his nose.

Only in ninth grade, though. They were placed in advanced sections by aptitude. But Bobby cheated down. Systematically worked to fail on tests and quizzes. Everyone knew. Those classes were full of kids cheating up — full of sideways glances and carefully dropped pencils, dates scribbled inside bandaids and formulas almost lost in sweating palms. And Bobby Giancaspro writing down the wrong answer, sometimes after showing the cheater next to him the right one. His C's and D's let him move, by tenth grade, to the comfort of classes where spitballs flew, where he gained a reputation as a back row mocker.

By tenth grade she had grown three inches more. She stooped through the halls, hopelessly bent by her armload of books, and it seemed she saw him only from enormous distances. But just before sleep sometimes, her breath shaky in the pillow, her body tensed against the bed, she found a moment when there was no space between them.

Now the sun is out but there's still a feeling of drip in the
air. Bobby has disappeared into the gas station and returns
with Nello, who looks more fat than tough in gray coveralls
and an unexpected John Lennon moustache. He glances her way,
Bobby says something, and she panics, regresses, feels her
glasses sinking heavy with scholarship on her nose, her knees
jutting into the glovebox, her arm a skinny dangle out the
window. She sits, big and quiet.

"Come in," Nello calls. "It's a moon party."

Timmie stuffs her glasses into her bag, shoves it under the
seat, and catches up as Nello leads them under the double
garage doors. He says the astronauts landed a while ago. They
go into the small back office where a couple of guys are
watching a tiny Sony TV. She leans against the desk and nods
to Glen Lenkowski, who wears bells and no shirt, and Dwight
Messerschmit, who is sitting on the floor in camouflage print
fatigues. She's never spoken to either of them.

At college, she has often done an imitation of their girls,
girls Bobby has gone with, Rona and Elena and Nello's sister
DeeDee, short tough girls with brown eyes and pale lips and
suede jackets shiny at the cuffs. She has found it's all a matter
of posture. You have to sink down into your hips and rock a
little — as now she rocks — and let the top of your head go
careless, put all the tension of enunciation into hip and jaw and
then you get the real New Jersey *yeah*. When she did it at
school, of course, they bought it; she would swagger *yeah* from
her pelvis, lift *yeah* with her chin, toss her hair *yeah* to
Boston boys who heard in it some Midatlantic promise of the
unrefined, but here, now, it is like speaking French among the
French and not in French class.

"You working around here this summer?" Nello asks her.

"Yeah."

"Want a Coke?" Bobby asks. "They got the Coke
machine in the shop unlocked."

"Yeah, sure."

Don't they see the tremors in her knees and elbows? But
they are watching the TV, where the mini-picture is a blur to
her without her glasses. She gathers that the spacemen are
just sitting on the moon; it may be hours before they get out and

walk. So she looks around — keeping the top of her head as careless as possible — at the metal shelves stacked with boxed parts, the rubber loops of fan belts on the wall, and, hanging right beside her, a big poster of a car stopped in a blizzard that reads: NEVER PICK UP A STRANGER — PICK UP PRESTONE ANTI-FREEZE.

"So what kind of job did you get?" Nello asks.

"Aaah, just selling jeans at the mall." She shrugs. "How've you been doing?"

As she and Nello talk they rock on their hips in unison.

When Bobby returns and hands her the bottle of soda, he feels impatient. Strange. Used to be when a day dragged the only way to get through it was hanging out in the back of Nello's with the guys. How often he drove around with them listening to a baseball game on the radio when each night stretched a summer long, grateful when somebody thought up stealing billboards or jumping the car across a brook. Now the time is gone and his best friends are assholes. He sees Timmie glance at Glen by the TV and remembers she scorned this at home, everyone just sitting around. She's right. There should be some better form of commemoration. He wishes they had gone to Eagle Rock. They could be there now, maybe see the moon rise and think how there are men on it, ending its solitude.

Nello is telling Timmie about his struggle with the draft. That's another thing. Here's Nello, poor bastard, flunking out of Paterson State, his last chance now in summer school, and what's he doing? Nello's doomed. You can see it in the rings of fat around his neck. His coverhalls are huge. And still he isn't fat enough.

"I can't get over 245, no matter what I try," he says to Timmie. "I can eat ice cream all day — I even made shakes of ice cream and beer — but 245 is my limit."

"How much do you have to weigh to get out?" Timmie asks. It bothers Bobby how she has settled in, sitting with her long legs crossed on Nello's dad's desk, among the empty carbon pads and lists of bad credit cards.

"I probably wouldn't be completely safe below 260. I thought I could, but I'll never make it. Even if I drink all the Coke in that machine."

"I think you can get diabetes if you just take in sugar all

the time," says Timmie.

"Can you get out for that?"

Bobby says, "Yeah, but it can make you blind."

"Well, forget that then," says Nello.

Timmie hesitates — Bobby sees she is about to say something but doesn't — and suddenly he doubts that diabetes causes blindness.

Nello goes on, "So I been taking Italian at summer school. 'Ecco, oona lettera por me. Chee sorpresa!' "

"Italy doesn't take draft dodgers, does it?" Glen asks without taking his eyes from the screen where there is a fuzzy picture of the moon craft sitting perfectly still. Glen is such an asshole, Bobby thinks.

"No. You have to be able to speak a language to go to translator school," Nello says. "Then they teach you Vietnamese or Cambodian or one of them."

"So how are you doing in Italian?" Bobby asks.

Nello shrugs. Which means, Bobby figures, with luck a D.

Timmie says, "I heard of a guy — it makes me think of you because I think he tried to get over the weight limit too — who got out by conditioning his blood pressure."

Nello looks at her expectantly.

Timmie becomes animated, the way she was in the car. "He conditioned his blood pressure to go up when they put on the, you know, the thing they take blood pressure with."

"How?"

"Well, he'd give himself a shock right when they pumped the thing up on his arm — not an electric shock, I think he just jumped into cold water or something. I guess he was liable to have high blood pressure to start with because he was so overweight. So when he had his draft physical his arm sort of *remembered* that this thing was associated with excitement and his blood pressure would go up to danger level, even though there wasn't any real shock this time. You see? It's called conditioned response."

"I could do that," Nello says. "Come on."

So they go into the shop and set up the Nellorelli Anti-Draft Conditioning Clinic. They fill the metal tub used to test flat tires for leaks and fish a piece of power steering belt out of the trash — "Although you should go to a medical supply place and get a real blood pressure taker because then you can know how much it goes up," Timmie tells them — and Dwight counts down "three, two, one," and Glen pulls the arm band tight and big Nello waves slosh the cement floor. Bobby tries to take part, all the time wondering why the others don't seem to see how carefully Timmie talks to them, talking down, just playing. The hem of her dress is splashed and clinging to her, and she laughs as they all count "three, two, one." Then a customer drives up and Nello, wet to the eyebrows, goes out to deal with him while the rest settle back by the TV.

Glen is onto one of those 'If we can put a man on the moon' kicks. Timmie — can she be taking him seriously? — is complaining, "It's not so much the money, but what's the point of the thing? You go somewhere, turn around, come back — so what?"

Bobby says, "But if you do something, you've done it. You always know."

She gives a shrug of assent. It's cool, with coolness of a different class than any coolness of his own. He feels too earnest. And yet he *was*.

Glen says, "But I mean, if we can put a man on the moon, why can't we solve world hunger?"

Nello, coming in and drying off with some rags, says, "Yeah, if we can put a man on the moon, why can't I learn Italian?"

And Dwight says, "Yeah, if we can put a man on the moon," grinning, "why can't I get laid?"

The guys roar. Timmie smiles. Bobby says to her, "You see? These guys are jerks. Think how long people have been looking at the moon, wanting to touch it. And now we have."

"But maybe," she says, "all we wanted was the shine of it."

"Yeah, maybe. Anyway," he says, "what's all this 'we' stuff? We're still all just sitting around in New Jersey."

Which makes them move. Nello is locking up the station. Bobby suggests they drive to Eagle Rock, but Nello wants pizza and then everyone wants pizza. They go outside. Glen and Dwight get into Glen's yellow Mustang with the spoiler and back seat speakers Bobby installed himself, back when the car was his. Bobby unlocks the Chevy. Nello gets in behind Timmie and calls over to Glen, "Let's see you lay some rubber, brother!" The Mustang peels out. Behind it, with a lurch that throws Timmie against her seat, Bobby drags a squeal from his mother's big damn boat of a BelAir.

By nine that night, when they turn in at Eagle Rock, they are an expedition. At the pizzeria they ran into Wilky, who had been class president and knew everyone's phone number, and now they have half a dozen cars, three cases of beer, girls, grass.

Though the night is cloudy, the clouds are high enough that as they round the curve to the lookout point they can see the classic New York skyline patterned in electricity. After Bobby parks, he and Nello and Timmie share a turn with the pay binoculars, Bobby trying to spot Edison's mansion in Llewellyn Park just below them.

As they walk over toward the old Casino where the rest have gathered, Nello gestures towards the city. "We had some royal times in that town, didn't we?"

Bobby says, "Yeah, Nel."

Nello puts his arm around Timmie. "He won't tell you. We, one time we went into the city with some of the guys from Wilky's band, you know that band he had for a while, they had a ton of money, and we got a suite at this hotel somebody knew — what was the name of that hotel, Bobby?"

"Can it, Nel," Bobby says.

"Why?" Nello turns to Timmie, "Wouldn't it be even better if I had the guys *throw* the water at me, like more of a surprise?"

"Good idea," she says. "Aren't you going to tell me about the hotel?"

"Oh, you know, we had them send some girls up, but shshsh, Bobby don't want to talk about it."

By now they are near the Casino. It was once, so their parents had told them, the night spot of the county, with dancing on the pavilion and light refreshments. In the 30's couples did the foxtrot here on chiffon summer nights and here, so they said, the young Sinatra sang, his voice crooning over Orange and Elizabeth, across the Jersey marshland and Hoboken his home, off towards the river and New York. The place was hit by lightning in the 40's, repaired, then hit again. Now a stone arcade is left, stone pillars, and a stone dance floor right out at the edge of Eagle Rock. The others have driven onto the grass and left their headlights on to light it for dancing. They've turned their radios up full blast.

Bobby leans against a pillar covered with spray paint memorials of Kenny + Patricia and Susie who loved Mario and a carved reminder that Phil was here in 1964. He wonders if Edison came up here — it would have been wild then, just a high rocky place and woods. Edison looked at the moon and saw a lightbulb. Was that what Timmie meant by wanting the shine?

Look at her right now, with Dwight showing her some step: shy, gawky. He thinks of the woman in the hotel Nello was talking about — his one such trip. He was 16. What he remembers is the way she washed herself, very tidily, and then made him wash himself and checked him, like a child. What he remembers is the angle of her legs as she washed herself, awkwardly squatted. Tired and remote. She was not cute, as all the girls he'd wanted were cute, and in that angle of her legs was contained his first fear that he was doing life all wrong.

A voice in the dark, a drunk male voice, is yowling, "Why d-don't we d-do it in the ro-ho-hoad?" even though it's the Temptations playing, and somebody is flashing headlights — no, they're waving something up and down over the headlights to make a strobe. He finds and loses Timmie, bits of her moving in the dance. Blinking against the stutter of darkness he assembles her, her hands flickering, the bright shake of her hair, her legs elongated in fractions of light.

Timmie has danced through music, through static, through the voices from the moon, has danced through Nello's Aretha Franklin imitation, danced with the whole crowd, doubletime soulclaps taking them faster, sometimes a beer flashing cold on her throat, danced until she can't breathe anymore and quits. She finds Bobby sitting with a group of guys at the front end of a car. The air is openly sweet with dope. Bobby is showing them how the moon goes around the earth with the headlight representing the sun and two tennis balls. He is trying to get them to believe the moon doesn't rotate as well as orbit. But some guy — she realizes she probably knew him in high school but now he's just like anyone else, bearded and strung out — keeps saying he can't tell them apart, they're both moons.

"Yeah, the earth shines too," Bobby says. "The light

bounces off us just like off of the moon."

"Where's it go?"

Bobby looks at Timmie with a laugh on his face. "Endless space."

"So they can see us?" the other says. Timmie thinks his name might be Roger.

"It travels," Bobby says seriously, "the speed of light. It takes a couple of hours to get to Saturn or Jupiter."

"So it's like pictures of us going into outer space?" asks Roger. "I think I saw a TV show like that once, where you could find nearly everything that ever happened out there somewhere, you know?"

Timmie sits on the bumper and puts her chin against her knees. She bums a cigarette off Roger, though she doesn't smoke. It's just this girl-gone-to-hell-smokin-on-the-corner-with-Nello's-sister-DeeDee mood. She lights it, lets it burn. Nothing to it — only, why couldn't she do it at fifteen?

Bobby has given the tennis balls to Roger, who is trying unsuccessfully to juggle them.

"Let's go ride around Llewellyn Park," Bobby says. "Let's find Edison's mansion down there."

Timmie asks if they don't have guards at the entrance to Llewellyn Park, but they are already on their feet, walking to the car, as he tells her there are back ways.

It feels late. She shivers, picturing the earth turning away from the sun, the warm skin of the planet cooling, and tennis balls in Bobby's hands. She asks, "So where are you in school now, anyway?"

He opens the car door for her. "I go to Glassboro State Teacher's College."

"Glassboro?" she says and then, ashamed to sound so snobby, she fumbles under the seat while he gets in — yes, her bag is there, her glasses.

"Oh," he says, "you remember Glassboro. Where Johnson met Kosygin because it was halfway between Washington and the U.N., making world peace right in New Jersey dairyland? The school commemorates the Glassboro Summit." His voice is mocking.

"Oh yeah, Glassboro, yeah," she says.

They glide down paths marked "No Motor Vehicles."

"Do you play football there?" she asks.

He tells her it took too much time. And when he lost his scholarship, his parents made him sell his car.

After a steep drop they are among rich houses. She is lost in the turns. Bobby pulls up by a turreted Victorian mansion. "Edison's house," he says.

"Are you sure it's the right one?"

"No."

They don't get out. They look across the lawn at New York shining. She thinks of herself there on Honor Society trips to the U.N. while Bobby and Nello were drinking, having girls sent to their rooms. But now she's different, he's so close she can hear him breathing. She tries to imagine what could possibly go wrong.

Bobby says, "When they put electric street lights in New York City, Edison could sit here and see it, all his lightbulbs lit. Think how dark it must have been, before."

They study the city's yellow allure.

"Do you think they'll put lights on the moon?" Timmie asks.

"Why not? Maybe it'll flash 'SMOKE CAMELS' and the man in the moon will issue puffs of smoke every thirty seconds."

"Maybe they'll just start with a giant 'THIS SPACE AVAILABLE.'"

He laughs and kisses her. When he touches her leg he touches right where it's painted, so she knows he has watched her. After a while he tells her — her mouth is hot against the nape of his neck — he hopes to transfer someplace good if he can make the grades. She moves to shut him up. A little later he has worked her dress up around her breasts, and she sits up and lifts it off and drapes it like a curtain across the windshield, using the visors to hold it in place.

"So the astronauts can't see us," she explains. She sits, leaning on the dash, while he lies across the seat.

"Yeah, they're really up there. On the moon."

Timmie inhales, doesn't speak. With her long hair concealing her face, her arms and legs look too elegant and cool. "What," he says, "what?" He rubs her back.

"I think it's sad," she says. "Poor moon."

"Ohhh, unAmerican." He pulls her down beside him. "Don't you know this is the land of go?" He presses her against the seat. He wants her to be awkward, he's glad it must be awkward there in the car. "Tell me, little hippie pinko spy, don't you believe in go, in get somewhere, huh?"

"Yeah," she breathes into his mouth. Their heads are pressed against the armrest. This close she can't see him; he is beer, sweat, lime. But still: *Bobby Giancaspro*. His hands are strong and the skin over his ribs, silky. So when he pulls on the elastic of her panties, she lifts. And when he asks, "Please, put your glasses on," she does, although it makes her shy.